FLESH AND BONE

Acclaim for Ronica Black's Fiction

Hearts Aflame

"Sleek storytelling and terrific characters are the backbone of Ronica Black's third and best novel, *Hearts Aflame*. Prepare to hop on for an emotional ride with this thrilling story of love in the outback."—*Lambda Book Report*

"*Hearts Aflame* takes the reader on the rough and tumble ride… The twists and turns of the plot engage the reader all the way to the satisfying conclusion."—*Just About Write*

In Too Deep

"*In Too Deep*, by newcomer Ronica Black, is emotional, hot, gripping, raw, and a real turn-on from start to finish, with characters you will fall in love with, root for, and never forget. A truly five star novel, you will not want to miss *In Too Deep* and will look forward to Black's next novel, *Wild Abandon*."
—*Midwest Book Review*

"Ronica Black's debut novel *In Too Deep* has everything from nonstop action and intriguing well-developed characters to steamy erotic love scenes. From the opening scenes where Black plunges the reader headfirst into the story to the explosive unexpected ending, *In Too Deep* has what it takes to rise to the top. Black has a winner with *In Too Deep*, one that will keep the reader turning the pages until the very last one."—*Independent Gay Writer*

"…an exciting, page turning read, full of mystery, sex, and suspense."—*MegaScene*

"…a challenging murder mystery—sections of this mixed-genre novel are hot, hot, hot. Black juggles the assorted elements of her first book with assured pacing and estimable panache."—*Q Syndicate*

"Black's characterization is skillful, and the sexual chemistry surrounding the three major characters is palpable and definitely hot-hot-hot…if you're looking for a solid read with ample amounts of eroticism and a red herring or two you're sure to find *In Too Deep* a satisfying read."—*L Word Literature*

Wild Abandon

"Black is a master at teasing the reader with her use of domination and desire. Black's first novel, *In Too Deep*, was a finalist for a 2005 Lammy…With *Wild Abandon*, the author continues her winning ways, writing like a seasoned pro. This is one romance I will not soon forget."—*Just About Write*

"If you enjoy complex characters and passionate sex scenes, you'll love *Wild Abandon*."—*MegaScene*

By the Author

In Too Deep

Deeper

Wild Abandon

Hearts Aflame

Flesh and Bone

Visit us at www.boldstrokesbooks.com

FLESH AND BONE

by
Ronica Black

2009

FLESH AND BONE
© 2009 BY RONICA BLACK. ALL RIGHTS RESERVED.

ISBN 13: 978-1-60282-093-7

THIS AEROS EBOOK IS PUBLISHED BY
BOLD STROKES BOOKS, INC.
P.O. BOX 249
VALLEY FALLS, NY 12185

FIRST EDITION: MAY 2009

THIS IS A WORK OF FICTION. NAMES, CHARACTERS, PLACES, AND INCIDENTS ARE THE PRODUCT OF THE AUTHOR'S IMAGINATION OR ARE USED FICTITIOUSLY. ANY RESEMBLANCE TO ACTUAL PERSONS, LIVING OR DEAD, BUSINESS ESTABLISHMENTS, EVENTS, OR LOCALES IS ENTIRELY COINCIDENTAL.

THIS BOOK, OR PARTS THEREOF, MAY NOT BE REPRODUCED IN ANY FORM WITHOUT PERMISSION.

CREDITS
PRODUCTION DESIGN: STACIA SEAMAN
COVER IMAGE BY LINDA SCOTT AND STEPHANIE K. YORQUE
COVER DESIGN BY BOLD STROKES BOOKS GRAPHICS

Acknowledgments

My heartfelt thanks to my beta readers, Lori, Jenny, Eva, and Kathi Isserman. Thanks so much for your advice and support. My thanks to my editor Cindy Cresap. It was a pleasure. Special thanks to photographer Linda Scott, cover model Stephanie K. Yorque, and graphic designer Lee Ligon for an incredible cover. And to Radclyffe, for allowing me to have way more fun than I should.

Dedication

We all have different definitions of love, eroticism, beauty, etc. The stories in this book represent mine, but many can be switched around to fit one's own definitions.
This book is dedicated to the process of that defining…
Oh, what a wonderful ride.

For the heart is an organ of fire.
—The English Patient

Contents

Introduction	1
F is for Fantasy	3
L is for Love	15
E is for Erotic	31
S is for Sensual	45
H is for Higher	71
A is for Animal	83
N is for Never	95
D is for Daring	109
B is for Beautiful	129
O is for Orgasm	143
N is for Naughty	163
E is for Everlasting	177

Introduction

F is for Fantasy
L is for Love
E is for Erotic
S is for Sensual
H is for Higher

A is for Animal
N is for Never
D is for Daring

B is for Beautiful
O is for Orgasm
N is for Naughty
E is for Everlasting

Flesh and Bone. What every woman is made of. Beautiful, daring, naughty, sensual. She has a fantasy, she wants to go higher, she searches for her own definition of love. She never says never, has her first orgasm, yearns for the everlasting. This is woman. You, me, the girl next door. We are all flesh and bone.

An eclectic collection of lesbian erotica, the stories in *Flesh and Bone* are as individual as every woman. From the sweetest petals of romance to the thorny edges of desire, our stories are as individual as we are. Yet one theme remains constant and keeps us intertwined: we are all Flesh and Bone.

F IS FOR FANTASY

She's on her way home and I'm ready but nervous. I wait by the door, fists opening and closing as if I'm waiting for the director to yell "action." My heart thuds, but so does my clitoris, the small cock in my jeans pressing against it. Both cause my hands and knees to tremble.

I'm trying to shake the jitters when I hear her car and peer out the window. She climbs out, slings her purse onto her shoulder, and heads for the stairs. Her heels click-clack and echo as she makes her way up. My heart seems to pump in tune with her steps.

Up and up she comes, like she's climbing to meet me for the very first time. I can recall it like it was yesterday, and I can recall that I was just as nervous.

I wait behind the door. Her footfalls stop and I can hear her digging around in her purse. She keeps the majority of her keys on a separate ring from her thick single car key. I know this about her and it does something strange to me. The familiarity comforts me, but knowing what it is I'm about to do to her both frightens and excites me.

The key slides into the dead bolt, and my heart lodges in my throat. The world around me slows, and I can envision the metal grinding of the key, the spark it creates as it meets and slides into its unique crevice. There's a heavy click, and my heart drops back into my chest again, the world rushing back in normal speed.

The knob turns and the door opens.

This is it. Now or never, now or never.

She steps inside and quickly I push the door closed and cover her mouth with my right hand.

Her muffled cry is one of shock and surprise, and I feel her body immediately tense. Her back is to me so I cannot see her face. I have no idea if she scared or intrigued.

"Don't move." My throat sounds raw and I can't believe I'm doing this. Can't believe it's happening.

She's silent for a moment, and all I can hear are my rapid breathing and the insane pounding of my heart. But then a long, single second later, she moans and it's long and deep and full of recognition and approval.

She knows. Oh God, yes, she knows. And she wants it.

I close my eyes, suddenly overcome with lust. My teeth find her earlobe, and the rose and sandalwood scent of her perfume shoots through my body. She thrusts her ass against my crotch and my eyes roll back into my head, overloaded with desire.

I remove my hand from her mouth as her purse and keys crash to the floor. She tries to turn to face me, but I don't let her, pressing her against the door instead. She exhales, misting the door, one cheek pressed just below the peephole.

"What are you going to do to me?" she asks.

I know what I'm supposed to say, but I find myself speaking with my body instead, forcing it full on against her. I lick her ear, around the outside to the inside. She reacts in an instant, like a bolt of lightning just shot up her spine.

The intensity, the raw desire, the quickness of our breathing, I'm into it now. Diving deeper and deeper. The words come surprisingly easy and they teeter in my mouth, balancing on the jagged cliffs of desire.

"I'm going to fuck you hard and fast. I'm going to fuck you hard and slow. I'm going to fuck you like you've never been fucked before."

Her breath hitches in her throat.

"Did you hear me?" Yes, I'm feeling it now. Demanding it. It's overwhelming.

She nods.

My hand trails down over her ass where I slip in beneath the skirt. Her cheeks are fleshy, yet firm and full. I smooth along the panties, pressing the fabric into her crack, teasing, testing. She wants me there, beckons me with her heat and her thrusts into my hand. But instead I move lower, going down to where her warm thigh muscles tremble.

"Don't move," I whisper. This fantasy, I realize, might as well have been mine.

The realization only stokes my inner fire more, to the point where if I don't escape the heat, I will burn. Hurriedly, I shove her skirt up. Her round ass is covered by lacy white boy short panties and accompanied by a white garter leading down to her sheer hose.

She has worn this just for me. Hoping that today would be the day.

My want for her suddenly becomes an ache. It hurts. It burns. It yearns.

I go to my knees and trail my tongue where my fingers have been, starting with her outer thigh and up to the outer edge of her panties. I kiss and nibble a bit and then push my tongue under the lace. She jerks and cries *yes*. But I leave her wanting and then do the same to the inner thigh, my tongue going up and pushing into the crotch of her panties.

She cries again and she's pushing herself back into my face. She's warm and moist, and I'm careful not to touch her most sensitive flesh, rimming the outside again and again.

She softly moans, trying to move. I hold her tight and stand. Again, I go to her ear and suck her lobe, holding it firmly between my teeth.

"Do you want it?" I ask. "Do you want me to fuck you?"

I flatten my palm firmly into her back and lick her ear again slowly, from the outside in.

"Say it," I demand. Oh, I know my lines well and I'm beginning to love the way they sound.

She mumbles in response, but I can't understand her. Instead of asking again, I unbutton my fly and urge the head of the cock against her, rubbing it in the crotch of her panties. Her cry is soft but sudden, and I press the head in further, giving her a good, long feel of what's to come. She moans and pushes into me, her palms on the door. I can feel the heat from her flesh against my fingertips as I tease her.

"Tell me you want me to fuck you."

I hear her breath hitch as she speaks.

"I want it. I want you. Oh God, I want it so bad."

Her words are searing hot swords. They fly into my ears and stab my brain. I feel dizzy and I hold her tightly as the cotton in my head begins to pound. It's different from the thud of my heart. It's heavy and foggy and charged with electricity, urging me on.

My fingers find her panties. Lace. Rough yet soft. Up and under I go to both cheeks, full of thick muscle and warm blood. I massage, squeezing and rubbing. And a strange noise arises from my throat.

Guttural want.

I tug down her panties. Nearly tear them in two.

A strange noise arises from her throat.

Guttural need.

Panties kicked aside, I hold her hips and watch her, cheek still pressed to the door. Her eyes are closed, her brow tense. Her coral lips are slightly parted, moist breath clouding the wood of the door. I lean into her, moving her thick dark hair from her neck. I kiss her there softly and allow her heated perfume to permeate my mind. It goes straight to my brain, then to my heart; in a lightning-quick flash, it's at my aching flesh.

I feel her heart beat, feel her breathing. My hands go down

and lift her ass cheeks. I slap them and she jerks, but then groans in pleasure. My hands go lower to her inner thighs where I urge her legs further apart. She complies quickly and I go down to my knees again. My tongue finds her hurriedly, licking up and down her thighs, up to her ass and back down again. Then up into her crotch where I rim her smooth, dripping lips. She bucks into me, voice crying softly. She's pleading. Begging. She's ready.

Standing, I slip two fingertips just inside her lips and she's hot and thick and slick. My eyes threaten to once again roll back into my head. She forces herself backward, trying to take in my fingers. I hold her still while I ready the cock, covering it in her slickness, stroking it up and down.

I'm hot and I'm long and I'm hard. My face burns with heat.

I lead the head to her lips and move it around, giving her another feel.

She says things I've never heard her say before. In a voice that sounds heavy and strained. "Please, now, I'll do anything, hurry, *now*, fuck, I want it, I have to have it, fucking hurry, oh God, fuck, please…" When her fist pounds the door, I do it.

I plunge into her.

Her cry is fervent.

And then there is silence.

Her breathing slows and her body feels tight like a stretched bow.

I stand very still, so turned on everything around us seems to melt away. This is her first time, and I know I must go slowly.

Deliberately, I run my hands under her blouse, undo her bra, and slowly and carefully I find her breasts. I tease them lightly and pinch the nipples, savoring the creamy soft feel of them, the slight weight of them in my hands. I whisper that I love her, and when her breathing increases again, I move.

Hands back on her hips, I pull away slowly and then push back into her. Her cry is blistering. I do it again. And again.

"Oh God," she says. "It fucking feels—ah, it burns. Burns so good."

I keep going, in and then out, in and then out. Fucking her long and slow.

"It's filling me. So full, ah, so much."

Her words and quick cries are music to my ears. And I keep on, until her hips are bucking back against me and she's panting with pleas for more.

"You want it?" I ask.

She can barely speak. "Yeah—yeah—yes."

I pump her harder and faster and ask if it feels good.

She can't seem to reply with words anymore. Only guttural groans.

I hear the smacking of the cock, the wet tightness of her pussy. The base of the cock is slamming into me, faster and harder, fucking my clit. Heat powerfully floods my face. I'm ready to go over. To not only tumble along with the surge of Niagara Falls but to actually leap off into it. And when she pushes back from the door, bends further at the waist, and holds tight to the doorknob, I dive headfirst into the crashing mist.

I come so hard my body seems to implode. My hands dig into her sides, my hips thrusting as hard and as fast as they can. I cry out, saying *fa-uuck* over and over again and she starts saying, "Yeah, baby, give it to me." She laughs a wicked deep laugh and says it feels so fucking good until "Mmm, mmm, mmm" is all she can manage.

I keep going, mind on overdrive, body ready to collapse.

Smack, smack, smack is all I hear.

She arches her back, offering more of herself to me. I take it wholeheartedly and thrust into her. Her moans eventually form one single word.

"Na-ow."

And then she screams, and it sounds like it came up from her fleshy core, through all the organs, into her chest, squeezed from her lungs, and forced out from her throat. It is the most beautiful sound I've ever heard and it seems to go on forever.

Teeth over my bottom lip, I keep pumping her. My own grunts sound foreign and my knees are threatening to buckle. She keeps coming. Long and deep and drawn out. One soul-bursting cry after another.

When she stops I don't notice at first. I'm caught up in my own reality, white sparks of pleasure floating around my head. She pulls herself up and leans against the door. I stop the thrusting and lean into her. We're both breathing hard. Her perfume seems heavier and hot, sizzling off her skin. It makes me dizzy.

We remain still for a few moments. Then, remembering her fantasy, I speak.

"Turn around." I ease myself out of her and she turns to face me. Her eyes are sparkling. The surface of a deep blue ocean lit by the teasing caress of the sun, the sparkles moving with the current, alive and alluring. Her cheeks are flushed, the skin of her neck a smeared red. Her lips seem thicker, full of hungry blood.

I take them with my own and she proves hungrier than I imagined.

I kiss her, using my tongue to explore hers. Her mouth is hot, searing hot. And suddenly I need to feel her center. To see if it too is hot and wanting to take me in. I reach down and soak my fingers in her come. Slick and thick and heated. I find her clit and frame it, squeezing the sides as I jerk her off. Up and down, up and down.

She grips my hair and bites into my shoulder.

"Uh, uh, uh."

Her clit grows, swells between my fingers. I move my hand faster. Side to side. Vibrate her. She claws my back, my scalp, and then leans completely into me as if she can no longer support herself.

I tell her, "Yeah. Come again for me, baby. Come so I can fuck you with my cock again."

Her head jerks back, mouth angled up to the ceiling. She comes in a brief cry, but her mouth remains open and silent as her body takes the rest of it. I bite down on the pulsing part of her neck, give her all I can. Her eyes are wide open, fixed on the ceiling, her face crumpling in sheer ecstasy.

Then she collapses upon me, body limp like a snapped rope. I hold her for a moment, kissing her neck, tasting her perfume mixed with her sweat. Oh, what an elixir.

Her mouth finds my skin, timid at first but then bold as she nibbles my neck. I so badly want to take her to bed, to lay her down and kiss her all over. To spend the night worshipping her with my tongue.

But the fantasy is not complete. And I know it's time to finish it. Bending at the knees, I lift her and carry her to the couch. She giggles mischievously and I lay her down and stand over her. I tear off my T-shirt and my breasts pucker from the cooler air. Her eyes almost close as her pupils dilate with desire.

I know this look. Would kill for this look.

I move closer and clench my teeth with nerve. Finally, I say it.

"Suck me."

After a long, seductive look, she props up on an elbow and grabs the cock. Her eyes remain locked with mine as she first licks it up and down and then takes it in her mouth. I watch her tongue; I watch her lips. My mouth begins to water. She's sucking me, swallowing me nearly whole. Her hand tugs on the shaft as she sucks. Again the smack, smack, smack.

Each one hits me at my core. A flamethrower triggering off my clit and firing into my body.

Oh God. Oh God, she's really sucking me off.

I hold her head. The feel of her bobbing back and forth intensifies the pleasure. She groans and closes her eyes. She moves faster, takes me deeper.

Oh God, I'm close. I'm so close.

I pull her head back. Her lips are parted, her eyes an abyss of sparkling blue.

I push her back and climb on. I reach to tear off her blouse. She groans her approval and lifts her arms so I can tug off the loose bra. Her breasts are cinnamon, centered in dark chocolate. My mouth takes them hungrily, tugging and sucking and biting. She calls out my name and arches herself into me.

I reach down for the cock. She starts to beg.

"Give it to me, give it to me."

She spreads her legs and with the cock in my hand, I feel her smooth, slick lips with my knuckles. Inward and upward I plunge.

"Oh God!" she cries out.

I feel her hips move beneath me and I plunge again as she claws my arms. She throws her head back in passion and I lick the straining tendons of her neck and push in some more.

The leather of the couch creaks and squeaks. I fuck her, fuck her good. And the fire in my own core burns hotter. My face flushes again. I'm close.

Head spinning, I sit back on my knees and pull the cock from her. Her eyes open in surprise and my hands go under her ass to lift her hips. I find her opening and wait, placing the head of the cock just inside. And then I plunge.

"Ah, ummm." She watches me as I fuck her.

I'm guiding her hips, yanking her to me, thrusting into her.

The heat spreads from my face down to my bare chest. My breasts sway as I move. My clit shoots fire into me with every thrust.

I'm close again. So close.

She begs for more, turning her head from side to side.

I go harder. I go faster.

"Do you like it?" I ask.

She moans.

I ask again. "Do you like me fucking you?"

She looks at me. "Yes. Yes, I like it."

"I'm going to come." I can't help myself. The sound, the feel of her under my hands, the pounding of my clit.

She throws her head back and lets out a high-pitched cry. I spill over the edge and tumble down, down, down.

Our bodies keep going. Fucking involuntarily. Fucking for sheer animal need.

We fuck we fuck we fuck.

And then we are still.

I lie on her. Breath ragged and coming quickly. Her skin is moist, her chest rising and falling, hungry for air.

The fantasy has been played out.

The sweet, sweet fantasy.

She seems to know my thoughts because she stirs. She pushes me back and I sit on my knees as she swings her leg around me to stand.

"Was it everything you wanted?" I can't help but ask, my mind just as spent as my body.

A thorny look comes into her eyes. She picks up her panties and comes back to me, pushing me onto my back.

"It was, yes. But now it's my turn."

"Your turn?"

She straddles me and carefully eases herself onto my cock. Her eyes glaze over. At first with hesitant intensity and then with incredible pleasure.

She leans forward, her face mere inches from mine.

"I'm going to have my way with you now."

She trails her panties along my face, hanging them over my mouth.

"Taste," she says. "Taste me while I fuck you."

She starts to move. Back and forth, to and fro. Her hand kneads my breasts. Presses into me for support. She moves faster. Her hips snapping.

She groans.

I reach for her breasts, massage them as she moves.

"There's more to this fantasy?" I ask, the fire building again as I catch the taste and scent of her on the delicate lace of the panties.

"Oh, yes," she says, stuffing them completely into my mouth as she quickens her hips. Her eyes flash with playful danger. "There's a whole lot more to this fantasy."

L is for Love

It started off simple enough. A cold, wind-driven night. The kind that makes you pull tighter on your already buttoned wool coat and hunker down against the curt, biting wind.

Gina Gordon was heading to the library for her Wednesday night scheduled reading. She was late and cursing up a storm, hands shoved into her coat pocket. Crossing the wet pavement, she hurriedly flung out her hand for the door and her keys came along for the ride, falling to the ground.

Mumbling another series of curse words, she bent and scooped up the keys. At that very moment, the door opened from the inside, knocking Gina back on her behind so forcefully that she bit her tongue.

"Ow, oh God," she said as she fingered her mouth. Her head spun and her tailbone seemed to have bitten into the ground.

Someone moved toward her, their colors trailing like a smeared painting or a fast-moving object. Gina blinked, but she had trouble focusing.

"I'm so sorry. Oh, shit. What did I do?"

The voice sounded familiar. Gina blinked again and took the offered hand. She stood on unsteady feet and allowed her vision to settle.

Melanie Macbeth stared back at her.

One doesn't forget a name like Melanie Macbeth.

Macbeth was Gina's favorite Shakespearean play.

And Melanie, lately, was quickly becoming another one of her favorite things.

Gina swayed. Or did she swoon? She wasn't sure.

Melanie was talking, but Gina couldn't hear. She often had this problem with Melanie Macbeth.

"Are you okay? Gina?"

Melanie's hand was insanely warm when it touched Gina's cheek. And the world seemed to rush around them, a record player on high speed.

"Yeah, I'm…" Normally she would've had something witty and clever to say. But the hand radiated and her tongue throbbed.

"Ow." Gina felt the wound and flinched. Blood quickly flooded her mouth, and she turned her head just as quickly to cough.

"Oh my God." Melanie bent down with her.

Gina, burning with more embarrassment than pain, tried to speak. "Get back. Don't wanna get blood on you." Only it came out sounding like her mouth was full of cotton. She coughed some more. Her face burned hotter. It was embarrassing. Very embarrassing.

"Here." Melanie gave her a tissue. "Hold this to your tongue."

Gina closed her eyes, unsure which she hated worse—the pain from her tongue, or the feel of the soft, dry tissue inside her mouth.

"Better?"

Gina stood. Melanie steadied her by cupping her elbow.

"We should get you inside."

Suddenly, the icy wind infiltrated her skin again. It surprised her. For those brief few moments, she hadn't been bothered by the bitter wind.

Melanie held open the door and Gina stepped inside. The

warmth of the library caved in on her and she found it difficult to breathe. Usually the warmth comforted her, but not now. Now it felt stifling and entrapping. Gina couldn't run away from Melanie even though she wanted, at that moment, to do nothing more.

Melanie was the head librarian and Gina saw her every Wednesday and sometimes on the weekends when Gina would come in and peruse the shelves. Lately she'd found herself searching for the meaning of the word *love*. In the books and in her everyday life.

That curious mission came to Gina's mind now, as Melanie quietly escorted them to the washroom where she encouraged her to sit on the low counter.

"Open," Melanie said softly, as if offering the sweetest, most sugary reward a child could dream of if she did so.

Gina fought off the nervous urge to swallow. She opened her mouth and had to close her eyes as Melanie took a closer look.

"Open a bit wider," she whispered sweetly. Gina opened her eyes and saw the penlight Melanie had dug out of her purse. Gina's heart rate kicked up as the scent of Melanie's gum mixed with her Obsession cologne.

"Now stick out your tongue." The words swirled like a warm, rum-tainted elixir.

Gina complied. She stared at the orange-brown maple wood of Melanie's eyes. Striated panels of beautifully stained wood, shooting from her pupils. Golds, oranges, browns. She stared at the paleness of her skin. Like moonlight on the darkest of nights. Her lips were like fragile pink rose petals basking in that incredible moonlight, just waiting for the right moment to open.

Gina was mesmerized. Normally, she didn't get such an opportunity to stare so blatantly at Melanie.

"It doesn't need stitches, so that's good," Melanie said, lowering the penlight. "The bleeding's finally stopped. There's some swelling, but that should be down by tomorrow."

"How do you know so much?"

"I read a lot."

Melanie smiled and held a warm, wet paper towel to her face. Gently, yet firmly, she cleaned Gina's chin, lips, and cheeks. Then she examined Gina's forehead and shone the penlight in her eyes.

"Do you feel dizzy? Nauseous?"

Around you? Always.

"Shih," Gina let out.

Melanie's back straightened and she looked alarmed.

"I'm sorreh. I mean…I wasn't talken to you." Damn, it really hurt to talk. And she felt like a fool. A blabber-mouthing, word-slurring fool.

What was she going to do? Words were her world. They comforted her, entertained her, and when she spoke them they protected her. Not being able to speak was for her like telling a mime he was a double arm amputee.

"Are you sure you're feeling okay?" Melanie looked worried.

Gina held her breath and felt her heart pounding furiously throughout her body. It was thudding, slamming, surging. All she could do was sit and stare, her senses electrified and seeking, taking everything there was to take in about Melanie Macbeth.

Her scent, so wonderful and warm. The splitting orange embers in her eyes. Melanie was like a quaint little cabin nestled in the blizzard-blown woods. Safe, warm, cozy. Shelter from the storm of life. Gina wanted to walk inside and never return.

She wanted to lie with her on a big bearskin rug, skimming over her firelit skin with her fingertips. She wanted to watch the small weight of her breasts pucker along with her lips. She wanted to take those lips into her mouth and…

"Gina?"

Gina refocused.

Melanie's brow was furrowed. "I'm worried. We should take you to the hospital."

"Wha? No." Gina stood. "I'm okay."

Melanie sighed. "I wish you would go in for a CAT scan. Just to be sure."

"No." Gina shook her head for extra effect and said as best she could, "Besides, I have a reading. I never miss a reading."

"That's true, you don't."

Melanie took Gina's hand and held it wrist facing up. Gently, she straightened her fingers and retrieved the wadded tissue. She threw it away and re-closed her fingers, giving her hand a slight squeeze.

"You're blushing," Melanie said.

"Oh." *Oh?* Gina cursed her cotton-stuffed tongue. She wished she could just tear open the seams and rip it all out.

Melanie didn't seem to notice. She handed her a paper cup full of water and told her to carefully rinse out her mouth.

"Better?" Melanie asked softly.

Gina swooned for real this time, lost in Melanie's eyes.

"You sure?" She steadied her, cupping her elbow.

Gina nodded, burned hotter, and then managed to speak. Sort of. "Mmm-hmm."

Melanie watched her for a moment and then gave Gina her coat and book bag. Once again cupping her elbow, she led the way through the door and headed into the main room.

The patrons were there, waiting for Gina by the big stone fireplace, many of them already comfortable in their chairs.

They all voiced hellos when they saw her. She gave a wave and smiled. Melanie led them to Gina's chair. It was dark green leather and positioned in front of the fireplace. A standing lamp and microphone flanked the chair, along with an ottoman where she always placed her book bag. Melanie offered Gina the chair and then sat next to her on the ottoman. Silence filled the room.

Gina was supposed to finish the John Irving book, but as she tried to say the simple word "hello" she knew she wasn't going to be able to do it.

Melanie was watching her. She smiled gently at Gina and then looked to the listeners.

"Ladies and gentlemen, Gina is unable to read to you this evening."

There were mumbles and grumbles. Someone asked why.

Melanie explained. "I hit her in the head with the door and she bit her tongue."

Gina did the oddest thing. She started to laugh. The whole scenario was really quite ridiculous.

"Since I'm the one who beat her up, I'm going to offer my services as a substitute reader for the night. That is, if you'll all have me. And..." She looked to Gina. "If that's okay with Gina."

Gina smiled. Then she nodded. She looked out at the crowd. Twenty-eight souls, give or take. Many had been coming to the Wednesday night readings for years.

She adored them. Just as they adored the words she shared.

Melanie found the book and opened to the marked page. She began to read.

Gina watched for a while. She studied Melanie's lips, the way they pressed and parted, the movement of the tendons in her throat, the graceful swoop of her neck. Then Gina closed her eyes and listened. Melanie's voice was like sugar. Thick, sifting handfuls of sugar. She imagined herself scooping up palmful after palmful and just letting it run through her fingers.

She imagined licking off the remnants. Imagined each tiny little granule melting on her tongue.

It was heaven. Sweet, sugary heaven.

And before she knew it, Melanie had stopped. The sugar canister had been closed. Gina opened her eyes and found Melanie watching her.

"How'd I do?"

Gina swallowed. "Good." She blushed again.

Melanie smiled.

Some of the listeners approached them, many of them talking to Melanie, who was always very kind and very patient.

And she touched them, not just emotionally but physically. She would cup their upper arms, or touch their faces and hands. She gave long, firm hugs, and yet she was as gentle as a lamb. She was wonderful. A wonderful human being.

"Are you ready?"

The question came out of left field. Gina tried to stop and rewind the past few moments. But she couldn't.

People were leaving, heading for home. Gina focused. Melanie was looking at her.

"We should really get you home."

Melanie swung the book over her shoulder and reached for Gina's hand.

Oh, how warm it was.

It was so warm that Gina barely noticed the harsh gale-like wind as it attacked them outdoors. All she could feel was Melanie's hand. Soft and warm and alive.

"You live in the Heights, don't you?"

Gina nodded. "How did you know?"

Melanie shrugged. "I've known for a while."

They rode in silence after that, in Melanie's Honda. Gina thanked her lucky stars that she didn't have to walk home, marching into the wall of frigid wind. Being with Melanie was better than she'd imagined. Warm, cozy, safe from the harsh cold. She felt like melting into the seat, and she found herself feeling disappointed when Melanie swung into a parking space and turned off the ignition.

"Here we are," Melanie said. And before Gina realized it, Melanie was at her door, pulling it open and helping her out.

They entered the building and the wind whistled through the outline of the doors.

Melanie smiled softly as they rode up the elevator and walked down the hallway to Gina's door.

As best she could, Gina asked if Melanie wanted to come inside.

Melanie studied her for a moment and nodded.

Gina opened the door and followed Melanie inside, hurriedly snatching up lingering water glasses and mail.

"I love your place," Melanie said, heading into the living room where two reading lamps shone from opposite ends of the couch. "These bookshelves are amazing." She ran her fingertips along the borders of the floor to ceiling shelves. "Did you have these put in?"

"I built them."

"Amazing," Melanie whispered.

"Would you like to sit down?"

Melanie walked to the sofa and held her hand out for Gina. There was a soft, inviting look in her eyes. "Sit with me," she said.

Gina sat and Melanie inched closer, laying her arm along the back of the couch. Her face was inches from Gina's, a warm crackling in her eyes. Gina could almost hear them. Feel their heat.

"We need to take care of you," Melanie whispered, leaning in closer.

Panic hammered with ferocity in Gina's chest. She closed her eyes, trying to get control.

She opened her eyes and Melanie pulled away.

"Is something wrong?"

"No." Gina said it as a whisper, her voice strained with desire. She stared into Melanie's eyes and felt her cheeks heat and her eyelids grow heavy with the sheer beauty of her. It was almost too much to take. Melanie was almost too much to take.

Melanie moved in again with a look of barely harbored hunger. Her knuckles brushed Gina's face. Their lips connected. Melanie's felt searing and pulpous and moist. So perfect and plump. Gina could taste her, smell her, breathe her in. She made her feel light-headed but hot weighted, like her head was floating above but her body was rooted to the couch.

Melanie kissed her gently. Oh so gently. Her lips framed and tugged on Gina's, her tongue carefully caressing, tickling, and tantalizing, very careful not to go inside where Gina was sore.

Her affection was saturating, sating every open lonely cell in Gina's body. Gina couldn't help but moan and knot her fingers in her shirt. Melanie responded by sucking her, first the top lip, then the bottom. Gina leaned forward with every tug, but then she leaned back, liking the feel of her pulling on her, liking the feel of being captured between her lips. After a short while, they both became breathless. "Do you know how long I've wanted to do this?" Melanie asked.

For the first time in years, Gina was lost for words.

"I've wanted you for so long," Melanie continued. "I should've asked you out, but the library is my job and I wasn't sure if I should." She touched Gina's face again, whispered her thumb across her cheek. "I've listened to you every night you've read. For months. Sometimes I even hid in the back to listen and watch. And somewhere along the way…" She turned her head.

Gina pictured her with the patrons. Touching their shoulders, holding their hands. Caresses so gentle, so kind, so caring that Gina seemed able to feel each one as if Melanie were touching her.

Melanie's cheeks plumed in dark pink patches. Gina touched them, felt the heat of what she was about to say.

"Somewhere along the way…" Her eyes were full of fire and Gina could see the pulse jump in her neck. "I think I fell in love with you."

Something invisible jammed Gina back into the couch and held her there. The cushions encased her. The pressure was so great she could hardly breathe. *Love. She said love.*

"I know it sounds crazy, but I can't describe it any other way. And tonight, well, tonight made it clear to me." Melanie watched her closely. Gina couldn't speak. No words were coming. Her vocabulary locomotive had run off its tracks.

"Do you think I'm crazy?"

Gina managed to swallow, shaking her head.

"No?" She exhaled against the delicate flesh of Gina's palm. "Are you sure?" Gooseflesh came to life on Gina's skin.

"Yes," Gina said. "I'm sure."

Melanie's kisses collapsed over her breath, pressing into Gina's hand. First with her lips and then with her hot tongue. She swirled it around and trailed up to Gina's fingers. In between, up and down. The sensation bolted hard and fast between Gina's legs. She pressed her thighs together and her toes curled.

She tried to speak, but Melanie stopped her by placing a finger to her lips. She leaned in toward her ear and whispered, "I want to show you how I feel tonight." The soft timbre of her voice trembled pleasure into Gina. Her body jerked, her senses intensifying every word.

"Please let me. I don't want you to do a thing. Just let me show you how I feel."

She kissed Gina's face. Oh, so lightly. One kiss here, one kiss there. Her breath was warm, her kisses awakening her skin.

"Can I?" Melanie said between each kiss. "Can I show you?"

She pulled away to look into her eyes.

Gina didn't know what to say or what to do. All she knew was that she wanted this woman. She wanted to know her, hold her, feel her. Love her.

Love.

There was that word again. *Am I in love? What does it mean to love? Why don't I know? Such a simple word, used in many different forms. I should know, but I don't.*

Melanie pressed another kiss to her lips. One that took her into an abyss of soft warmth with silk and satin all around her, caressing her, encasing her, threatening to take her away forever.

She looked into her eyes again and they both were struggling for breath. Gina realized that her body felt electric and alive, every nerve tingling and aching for Melanie. Like a plug craving a power socket, Gina pressed her lips to hers and felt the surge of her energy.

Gina's brain and body screamed. Insisting.

"Yes," she managed in between kisses.

They pulled apart and an amorous smile spread across Melanie's face. She stood and held out her hand. She led Gina to her bedroom and flicked on the bedside light. Her eyes swept up and down her body, then Gina watched her hands as they began unbuttoning her blouse. Gina tried to help, but Melanie held her wrists and shook her head.

"Let me," she whispered.

Inch by inch, Gina's shirt was loosened and opened. Her heart ricocheted behind her ribs and her breath hitched when Melanie's knuckles skimmed her flesh.

Gina's every cell was open and waiting. Craving her.

Melanie pushed the blouse off her shoulders and sank her teeth into Gina's neck. Her mouth burned and bit as she kissed and sucked, fastening herself to her. *Oh God.* The rush was bliss, the intensity weakening her knees. Melanie's feeding frenzy found its way to her ear where she told Gina how wonderful she tasted, how she loved the feel of her skin yielding beneath her. Her fingers dragged down to Gina's slacks where they unbuttoned and unzipped. As soon as the pants were open, her hand sank inside her panties where she stroked her.

"Oh God, yes. You're so wet, so very wet." She bit her neck again, cooing to her. Her hand was nestled in her folds, moving up and down, encasing her clit with her silky desire.

Gina couldn't speak. All she could muster were strained moans of approval.

"I'm so sorry," Melanie said, "I just couldn't wait. Oh God, you feel so good."

Threatening to collapse in ecstasy, Gina gripped her wrist and stilled her hand. Melanie seemed to understand.

"Right, okay. The pants." She tugged them down, along

with her panties. Then her eyes took Gina in as she hurriedly tore herself from her own clothes. She stood before her, eyes ablaze, breathing rapidly, and Gina noticed that the pink splotches on her cheeks matched those that marked her chest. Melanie was aroused, her skin alive and vibrant.

Gently, she eased Gina onto the bed. The pain from her tailbone slammed through her like vibrating symbols. Melanie cupped her face with her hands and kissed her tenderly.

"I'm sorry," she whispered. "Why don't you lie on your stomach?"

Gina hesitated, but Melanie's eyes melted her resolve.

"Go ahead," she whispered, trailing her lips down to her neck.

Her skin electrified, Gina turned and lay down, resting her cheek on her pillow. Her head sank lower and she could hear the racing of her pulse echo throughout the thick cotton.

Melanie whispered to her again, but she was unable to hear. And then Gina felt her hands. Warm and firm, rubbing over her back. Then fingertips skimmed where the hands massaged, feather light and awakening from her shoulders to her backside. Gina quivered, each skin cell wanting to reach out and grab her hand.

Melanie kept whispering, her words stroking Gina like her fingertips, in circles, large and small, long lines up and down her back. She traced and trailed, tickling and teasing. Gina felt her move, felt her fingertips flatten into palms. Then Gina felt the soft furnace of her mouth. Kissing, pressing, and releasing. First hot and wet and then vacant and cold as the night air assaulted where her mouth just left.

Careful, slow, deliberate, Melanie followed the path of her hands, covering every inch. Gina's body jerked and settled, jerked and settled. Gina clenched her pillow, cried out into its soft depths.

Her mouth continued downward, lightly kissing her buttocks. Again she made the circles, this time with her tongue. Gina felt herself tense. Felt her fingertips run up and down her thighs. Melanie's lips collapsed over her tongue and she kissed her, careful to avoid where she was most certainly going to bruise. The kisses were harder now with her tongue fully involved. Down she went. Over her buttocks to her thighs.

Kisses. Hot kisses. Hard, pressing kisses.

Swirling tongue kisses. All over her thighs.

Her hands moved down farther, charting the way for her mouth. Down to the backs of her knees and beyond to her calves. Her mouth followed quickly, her desire no doubt growing. Gina could hear her moaning now. Hear the sharpness of her breathing.

Gina jerked at the tickle of her attached to her inner thigh. Nearly came off the bed when she kissed the bend of her knee.

Melanie laughed and nibbled on her. Ran her nails down the outsides of her legs.

Then she stopped. Gina felt her move and her hand cupped her hip as she encouraged her to turn over. Gina found Melanie's face more flushed than ever. Her breasts were rising and falling with her breathing. She kissed Gina's lips only briefly and Gina was able to catch the baked coconut scent of her hair. It tickled her as she worked her way down once again, across the planes of her stomach, down to her pelvis where her tongue extended to trace around her trimmed hair. Gina's mind panicked but her body surged with white-hot yearning. She told her to wait but her hips disagreed, lifting toward her mouth.

"Let me," she said. "Just let me."

Gina wasn't nervous. No, that wasn't the word. She was unsure. And she felt exposed.

Oh God!

Melanie was kissing her, skirting her hair. With every imprint of her lips, she shushed her, saying, "It's okay. Let me love you."

Then Melanie nestled her body between her legs and spread her open with her palms. Gina lifted her head to look at her, to tell her to wait once again. But she was already at her, tongue licking up her thigh to her center. Her thumbs moved from her thighs to her lips, where they spread her open further, dipped into her arousal, and then rubbed her clit.

"Oh God," Gina breathed. "Oh God."

Melanie grinned at her and then pressed her face to her center. Gina felt her tongue rim her entrance and then felt it shoot inside her, pushing and thrusting. She squeezed the bed covers and slammed her head into the pillow. Melanie's thumbs continued, playing her clit like a well-tuned guitar. Both sides, on the top, inward and outward, up and down.

Oh God. Oh God.

And her tongue, swirling, pushing, in and out and all over again.

She's...she's...oh God, she's fucking me with her tongue.

Gina couldn't think. It felt so good. It felt so good. She couldn't get past that. Couldn't get past how good it felt.

"Please," Gina managed, once again lifting her head.

Melanie stopped and met her gaze. "Please what?"

Breathing heavily, Gina fell back into the pillow.

Melanie was still watching her. Gina could feel it.

"Please don't stop?"

Her thumbs started again. Playing her magic core.

Gina jerked and groaned.

"Okay, I won't stop."

Gina looked at her and watched as she went back down.

Melanie's tongue shot into her and her thumbs quickened.

Gina's back arched and her groans turned to deep, throaty cries.

She closed her eyes and felt her body start to float. She opened them and stared at the ceiling. *Yes, yes, I am floating.* The ceiling focused and unfocused. It grew closer and closer.

Gina's body was humming. Existing on a plane she never could've imagined.

She felt herself thrusting into Melanie, her fingers tangled in her hair. She didn't know how or for how long. Reality was gone, lost in a haze of humming pleasure.

The ceiling loomed closer.

Closer.

Closer.

And then Melanie said it. Said it so quickly Gina thought she imagined it.

She said, "Love."

Just "Love."

And then it happened.

Gina reached the ceiling and it imploded.

Into the most brilliant of bright lights.

Electric reds and blues and purples and yellows.

All of them representing raw pleasure, raw pleasure humming and swirling into one another.

She clung to her head and watched the colors come down and consume her.

Pleasure, pleasure, *oh God,* pleasure.

Gina opened up, took hold of it, squeezed it, and never wanted to let it go.

She held it and held it.

Held her.

Felt her body vibrate and flex and vibrate and flex.

And then Melanie's head lifted and she looked at her.

Gina could hardly catch her breath. Melanie was flushed in different shades of pink. Her lips were full and darkened.

"I love you, Gina. I can't help myself. And I…" She looked down to her thumbs. "I love this." She dipped them once again into her arousal and pushed them into the sides of her clit. She began to massage again. "I love giving you pleasure. Watching it overcome you. I love it. I love it all."

Gina's hips bucked.

Oh God. It was starting again.

"Oh, yes, Gina. Take it. Take me. Let me love you."

She was playing her, all so perfectly. The rhythm of her touch was dangerous. So good and so dangerous.

And as the colors on the ceiling called out to Gina once again, all the words she'd ever read on love made sense. And yet they didn't come close to describing the magnitude of her feelings.

Love, love, oh God, I desperately need words to explain it...

She cried out. Cried out so loud her voice weakened and caved.

The colors swirled, her body burned, her nerve centers took took took.

Her heart rejoiced.

All of it happened and happened together. It lasted, a glowing ball of mingling energy, it lasted for a very long time.

And Gina looked at her after she stilled.

Her eyes. Her pink flushed skin. The sweat along the dips of her collarbone.

A tear welled and fell down Gina's cheek. She smiled but hitched with a cry.

"I love you," Melanie said, coming forward to brush at her cheek.

And suddenly, the words came to Gina. Love could not be controlled or contained. Could not be truly taught or truly explained. It was the great mystery of life, the great necessity, the greatly desired, the grand ride along the way. There were no answers, no words to encapsulate it. It just…simply was.

Gina nodded and reach for her hand. She held it to her heart and said only what she was able to say and what she'd never thought she'd ever have reason to say.

She said, "I love you."

E is for Erotic

The sun is sick with gray, the sky a hazy pewter screen. Around her the street drones to the rhythm of the passersby. People talking, walking, hurrying, cursing the downpour. Cars swishing, horns honking, wipers whining, whipping across pelted windshields.

Her thick, white high heels join in, click dully on the wet pavement, weaving expertly between people and puddles. The air is heavy with chill and she breathes it in deeply, welcoming the taste and feel of the cold rain. It's fitting, yet invigorating.

Heart and feet beating with a purpose, she sinks her hands into the deep pockets of her large raincoat, searching for her music. Finding a tiny earphone, she pops it into place and pushes Play from her pocket, leaving the iPod safely inside.

Her eyes drift close momentarily as the drums, violins, and harp all start up, setting her mind into the mode of her purpose.

She opens her eyes and focuses on the tall building not far ahead. She counts the floors downward from the top. Julia is on the sixty-fourth.

Eyes trained on the building, she hurries, anxious and excited. There is something she must do on this cold, rainy Wednesday. Something that cannot wait any longer.

Her heels click on, carrying her on the wings of the beautiful Celtic music. When she reaches the building, she stops in front of the large doors and looks up into the falling rain. She takes in the sharply vertical skyscraper and closes her eyes. The raindrops melt into her skin and run icy fingers through her scalp, grounding her with the chill, soaring her with the thrill.

Yes. It's all making sense. It's good she's here.

She pulls out the earpiece and embraces the static hum of the world around her. The doorman calls to her, people sidestep her, "excuse me, lookout, pardon me," all of them a weaving snake of bobbing black umbrellas. Rain thumping down on it all, whispering in her ear.

Julia.

Growing a little dizzy, she steps inside the building, making her way immediately to the elevators. Yellow tent signs warn CAUTION WET FLOOR. And the large lobby smells of damp polyester and dirty streets from the hundreds of pairs of wet shoeprints.

Dozens of people clamor by, exiting like packed cattle from the elevators, all of them on a mission called "lunch." Bobbing and dodging, she manages to find an elevator going up.

"What floor?" a nice-looking man in an expensive business suit asks, his slack umbrella dripping onto the gray Berber carpet.

"Sixty-four," she says, breathless.

Beside her a woman shuffles away tow--- --- --- and a few people behind her clear their throats. A cell phone rings in the tone of a dog barking "Jingle Bells." Someone chuckles and another sneezes.

The elevator stops three times on its way to sixty-four. Men and women squeeze by her, hurrying off to their appointments or their desks. She pushes up the arm of her coat and glances at her watch.

Five till noon.

Perfect.

Sixty-four arrives and she steps off, glad to be in the open but nervous about the destination ahead. A maze of cubicles challenges her, but she moves quickly, giving the few heads she does see little attention. Phones ring and beep, most of them going unanswered. When she reaches a main corridor, people smile and nod, rushing by her. A few stare and one even comments on the rain. She smiles but lowers her eyes, quickening her step.

When she reaches Margaret's desk she's glad to see that she's already left for lunch.

She looks beyond Margaret's area to the blinds on Julia's windows. They are vertical and closed, and as she approaches, she's just able to make out Julia's voice on the other side. Hand on the cool doorknob, she closes her eyes and leans in, listening to the deep, throaty strum of her. Julia's voice was the first thing she'd been exposed to when they met. A business phone call that had been placed across the wires and into infinity nine years ago. That phone call had led to many, many more.

And now they are here. In this moment. Her heart beats wildly into her throat as she turns the doorknob. Opening her eyes and breathing deeply, she eases the door open. Julia doesn't see her at first, facing the large outer window overlooking downtown, phone pressed to her ear. She steps inside, takes another courage-seeking breath and leans back against the door as it closes, making sure to lock it as well.

The click catches Julia's attention and she turns. Her blue eyes widen and her face halts with true surprise. A low whisper escapes her. "Sam." Then, caught back in the net of conversation, she continues.

"Ye—yes, I understand."

Sam doesn't smile and she doesn't wave. Instead, she crosses briskly to the broad oak desk and pulls the book bag from her shoulder. She busies herself retrieving the items she needs. Three wide candles, a small book of matches, her iPod, which she sets in Julia's speaker stand, and one single white rose.

Julia watches her closely, saying "mmm-hmms" into the phone. Sam's body heats under her stare and heats even more under her unspoken questions. Sam meets her gaze, promising answers and a whole lot more.

The match scrapes and snaps to life as she lights the candles and places them along the front of the desk. Then she walks to the big window and closes the blinds. The room immediately comes to life, inhaling and exhaling with the breaths of the candlelight.

Sam gets lost in it for a moment, her body buzzing, her soul rooting and growing in what it is she's about to do. With a false sense of confidence, she stands in front of her lover of eight years, her best friend of nine. Julia's eyes search hers desperately, and Sam can see her pulse in the tiny vessel on her temple.

"Say good-bye," Sam whispers.

Julia clenches the phone. "Right, right. Yes. Listen, Bob, I need to run. What's that? Yes, okay. Uh-huh. Okay. Talk to you soon. Good—"

Sam unplugs the phone, simply pulling the cord out from behind the charging stand. Julia lowers the receiver slowly and Sam takes it and sets it in its cradle. Julia still appears too shocked to speak.

"Hi," Sam offers, taking Julia's hands in her own.

"Hi." Julia holds up her hands. "You're freezing." She looks at her face and the shoulders of her coat. "Soaked nearly through. I'll have Margaret get you some coffee."

"She's gone," Sam says. "Just as nearly everyone else is. Besides, I'm far from cold."

"Did you forget your umbrella?"

"Didn't want one."

"Why not?" Julia still sounds confused.

"Because I wanted to feel every drop." Sam made sure to look into her eyes.

"You did?"

Sam runs her hands through her hair, finger-combing her long, dark locks. "Yes."

"I don't understand—are you okay?"

Sam once again holds her stare. "No. I'm not okay. Because *we* haven't been okay. But I'm about to make that right. I'm about to show you just what it is you do to me. What it is you mean to me."

"I'm so sorr—" Julia tries.

"No. Don't speak. Please. We are long past words. Spoken or unspoken. And we are long past meaning well and meaning to. It's time to *do*." She takes her hand and pulls her in front of the chair and then pushes her down into it.

"Sit," Sam says, inches from her lips. "And don't move." Julia nods and Sam wheels the chair around the desk face-to-face with the visitor's chair. Julia tries to speak again, but Sam stops her lips with a press of her finger.

"Shh."

Sam leans against the desk and pushes play on the iPod. She adjusts the volume for Loreena McKennitt's "Marco Polo." Beautiful, haunting, and exotic, it is Sam's narrative for Julia. It gripped her the very first time she heard it, just as Julia's voice had.

Allowing the music to fill her, Sam stands in front of Julia and unties the belt of her raincoat. Then her fingers undo the large buttons. Julia's cheeks bloom red and her hands squeeze together in her lap. Sam can tell her breathing has quickened by the rise and fall of her chest.

The music is a hypnotic instrumental and Sam knows every bit. She runs her hands down the front of her raincoat to ease it apart, her entire being filling up with Julia, her voice, her eyes, her face, her hands, her song.

"I love you," Sam whispers, opening the raincoat, slipping it from her shoulders and letting it drop to the floor.

Julia tries to mouth it back, but Sam stops her, bending to gather her lips in her own for a quick, heated kiss. Sam feels her tense but then soften, and a low groan comes up from her chest.

Sam massages her lips softly, wanting desperately to continue, but she pulls away, very much aware of her own body's burning-hot need. The scent of Julia, the feel of her lips, the sound of her groan…it had been so long, so damn long. Her body and soul had been so empty, like a cold, parched fireplace that had just been stacked with thirsty logs and hungry kindling. Lit matches were now being tossed into it, end over end.

Whoosh. She can feel the sudden heat and flame, hear the snapping and crackling of her own burning desire.

She wants her, needs her, and she stands before her, wearing nothing but white lace panties and a matching bra. Julia's favorite.

Her skin feels alive as if Julia had run her nails lightly over her.

"I can feel you," she says to her, the fire surging. "I've been feeling you since early this morning."

Julia watches her, the blooming on her cheeks darkening.

"I was in the shower when it started," Sam says breathlessly, trailing her fingers up and down her sides, moving her hips to the music. "I was out of my shower gel so I picked up your soap and started lathering myself. And the second I caught the scent of it, I nearly collapsed. The smell of it, of that sudsy, curved white bar… it was you. And it had been so long since I'd inhaled the silky, soft scent of your skin, it nearly overwhelmed me. Especially when I realized…that it was you I was rubbing all over me."

Julia swallows and her pulse races along side her throat. Sam steps up to her and straddles her, laying her legs over the armrests of the chair. Gripping the back of it, she arches her back and thrusts her chest forward. "See, baby. Smell me. I have you all over me."

Sam looks to the ceiling, watches the shadows flickering there, and moans when Julia's breath finds her collarbone. It's followed quickly by her warm hands, palms flattened against the planes of her back, rubbing up and down. Julia inhales and exhales, electrifying Sam.

"Oh God, Julia," Sam whispers. "You feel so good. You touch me everywhere. Do you know that?" She holds Julia's face in her hands, feels the fire of her skin. "No matter where you are in the world, you're always touching me all over."

She kisses her again, this one longer and deeper as their tongues probe hungrily. More noises come from Julia and her fingers dig into Sam's back. Sam wants so badly to give in and ravage her right away. But she forces herself to push away, to break her lips away from Julia's.

Standing, Sam dances some more, skimming her hands over her body, holding Julia's gaze. The music seems to crawl inside her, captivating her muscles, moving through her like a wave. She closes her eyes, licks her lips, imagines Julia is touching her...everywhere, inside and out. That her mouth is upon her, those luscious lips, the long pink tongue.

Sam glides her hands to her bra. She frames her lacy nipples, rubs in circles, exciting herself. The sensation bolts straight down her body to her clit, and Julia's eyes upon her as she does it only intensifies the moment.

Trembling with desire, Sam moves her fingers to the straps of the bra. She slips under them, bringing them down from her shoulders. Then, holding Julia's gaze, she reaches back and releases the clasp. The bra slinks down her arms and falls slack at her side. She drops it to the floor. And once again she moves her hips and hands, touching and teasing, all the way back up to her breasts. She frames her now bare nipples and squeezes, delighting in the spark it causes between her legs. She does it several times, tensing and hissing, clenching her eyes and then opening them in amorous surprise.

Julia watches it all from the chair, her back straight as a rod, her face flushed, and her hands holding tightly to the armrests. She sits very still but her eyes are a fiery blue and her lips are a swollen deep red. She swallows frequently, her lower lip twitching and sometimes mouthing silent words.

Sam can smell her skin, that hot, silky, sudsy smell, and she knows she's aroused. Just the look of her, sitting so intently, perched like a cat hunting in tall grass, ready to pounce at any second. It makes Sam wet.

So much so that she decides to show her.

Sliding her hands down, Sam slides them under the lace of her underwear and lowers the fabric to her ankles. She steps out of them carefully and retrieves the white rose from the desk.

The soft petals kiss her nose and then her lips as she inhales. Julia watches her closely and her eyes dilate when Sam sits in the chair directly across from her.

"A white rose," Sam says. "Your favorite." She presses it to her lips again and smiles. "You always say you love the way they smell, the way they feel on your skin."

Sam runs the rose over her chin, down her neck to her breast. There she twirls the satin swirl around her erect nipple, hissing at the sensation. "You're right," she says. "It feels so good. Just like you." Slowly, she traces the rose down her abdomen to her pubis, her muscles trembling at the faintest of touches.

Body on fire, she inches back on the chair and spreads her legs up and over the armrests. Julia tenses and her eyelids appear to grow heavy as her irises focus in desire. Sam warms at the sight, and her nerves feel charged as if throbbing with neon.

She feels so out of control, everything inside and out of her reacting involuntarily. She's aching and aching, wanting to show and take.

She concentrates on the candlelight as it flickers across the room. It shadows the elegant features of Julia's face, creating two halves. One light, one dark. One full of immeasurable love and devotion, the other full of incredible lust and desire. Both of them staring her down.

The music strums along with it all, stroking the air with tangible vibrations causing the rose to almost move along on its own, following the music's path, weaving intricate designs along her skin.

When the soft petals reach her bare, aching flesh, she inhales sharply. Julia leans forward, the veins in her neck and hands standing at attention.

Sam mumbles in pleasure, stroking the rose along the sides of her clitoris. Making great grand circles around and around. She can feel herself throbbing, dying for the pressured touch directly on her reddened knob. She sighs into the dancing light, moves her hips up and around at the music. The satin swirl of the rose works its magic mystically, and when she pushes it upon her clitoris she arches her back and cries out in ecstasy. Twirling and twirling, she presses it firmer and firmer against her. Pulsing in pleasure, she tightens her abdomen and holds her head off the chair, locking eyes with Julia.

"This is what you do to me, Jule. Do you see it? Oh, oh God, it feels good." She brings herself close to climax, so close she can feel every tendon in her body strain for it.

"Look," she says, forcing herself to go slower. "Look at how wet…"

She lowers the rose to her opening, feels the teasing of the tightly wound petals as she dips the tip inside. Somewhere, amidst the music and the glimmering light, she hears Julia groan.

"Yes, Julia," she says. "This is how you make me feel. See it. See it all." She twists it and dips it, fucking the tight, soft petals, saturating it with her arousal.

"Oh, honey. Yes, oh God. I'm fucking your rose. I'm fucking you. Do you see it? I'm so wet, look, Julia."

"Ah," Julia mumbles. "You're so beautiful."

Sam brings the rose upward, trailing her hot, silky wetness across the planes of her belly, up to her breasts, where she once again spins the rose upon her nipples.

"See, baby? See how wet I am?"

Julia groans a yes and then drops to her knees. She wraps her hands under and around Sam's thighs, holding her close. Sam stares into her fiery eyes, feels Julia's breath searing her skin. Sam wants to follow those breaths, hold them captive, and then crawl in after them. Using the rose, she touches Julia's lips. Julia inhales deeply and then kisses it, extending her tongue for a taste.

"My two favorite smells," Julia whispers, rubbing her cheek along the rose, closing her eyes. When she opens them, she takes the rose from Sam and skims it along her skin, up one thigh and down the other. Sam jerks and sighs, watching and feeling. Julia plays with her like that for a bit longer and then brings it back to Sam's center where she places it top down upon her clitoris. She spins it carefully and lowers herself, once again extending her tongue, this time to find Sam's opening.

"Oh God," Sam murmurs, gripping Julia's thick, sandy mane, the feel of her heavy wet tongue driving her mad.

Julia thrusts inside her and Sam throws her head back, the slick, firm tongue delving in and twirling around and around just like the rose on her clit. Noises come from them both, short, sharp gasps and long, throaty growls. Sam begins to pump her hips, the ecstasy building and building. In a hurried motion, Julia tosses the rose aside and brings her mouth up to feed where the rose had been. Then long, hard fingers tease Sam's opening just before Julia shoves them inside.

"Oh God!"

Julia's pumping her. Into her, out of her, fast, hard, long, and short. Her mouth is now sucking, sopping Sam's clit in a confinement of wet, soft lips and dense, slick tongue.

"Fuck, oh God, Julia. Baby—" Sam shuts her eyes, the mounting pleasure too great. The music strums, beats, and moves in its hypnotic rhythm. The candlelight matches it, pulsating, beating, and dancing. Her insides do the same, reflecting her outside. Strums, beats, pulsations. All of it doing so with one word.

Julia. Julia. Julia.

Sam calls out her name then, loud and deep and throaty, hands clinging to her head, body shoving into her. Julia groans in return, tightening her grip, fucking Sam harder and harder.

"I can feel you—" Sam stutters. "I can feel you filling me.

All of you, all over me. In me and on me. You. Everywhere. I love you—"

Her body rocks and shakes and then stills. The million little pieces of her fall slowly and gently back down, like spent confetti.

"Julia," she says one more time.

Sam lies there, body limp, mind flaccid. Julia lifts herself, but leaves her fingers inside. She grins slightly, her blue eyes soft, her mouth swollen, her skin bloomed in red.

Sam grins back but feels the pooling of tears in her eyes. "I love you," she says, noticing that the music has stopped.

Julia stares into her eyes. "I know. I mean, I really know."

Sam touches her face. "Good."

Julia lays her cheek on Sam's abdomen. "I'll never forget this." She looks at her. "Thank you."

"No," Sam says. "Thank you."

A knock sounds from the door, startling them both. The doorknob turns back and forth quickly but to no avail.

"Julia?" It was Vinny, Julia's protégé.

"Shhh." Julia laughs. "Maybe he'll go away."

Sam sits up, holding fast to Julia's wrist. "I wish he would."

Julia gives her a smoldering look and leans in for a tender, delicate kiss. "He will." She moves her fingers deep inside Sam, causing the sweet burning pressure to return.

More knocking. "Are you in there? Are you okay? I smell smoke."

Julia groans in obvious frustration. "I'm fine, Vinny. Give me a moment, okay?"

"Doesn't he go to lunch? I thought at least we'd have the hour."

"Vinny doesn't eat. He doesn't sleep. He's a machine."

Sam grins lazily. "Like you?"

Julia kisses her again and removes her fingers. She stands and brings Sam with her.

"Maybe. But a different kind of machine."

Sam laughs. "I'll hold you to that, then."

More knocking. "Julia, I'm really sorry, but Tokyo is on the line—"

"Okay, Vinny. I'm on it." She touches Sam's face. "I'm sorry."

"It's okay."

"Not really."

"So make it up to me."

Julia raises an eyebrow as Sam slips back into her cold, damp coat.

"Come home at a decent time tonight. And spend the weekend with me." She stuffs her bra and panties into her book bag, along with her iPod.

"Okay. I will."

Sam shivers and stands before her. They exchange another soft kiss.

"I love you so much," Julia says.

"I love you too."

Julia glances at the candles. "What about those?"

"Keep them. They smell good and they'll remind you of me." Sam picks up the rose. "Along with this." She presses it lightly to Julia's lips. "Save it always."

"I will."

Sam walks away, tears in her eyes. When she reaches the door, she turns and smiles.

"See you tonight."

Julia nods, rose under her nose. "Tonight. And forever."

Sam tugs the door open and Vinny nearly stumbles in. He smiles and greets her but then suddenly blushes profusely. Sam leaves him confused and walks in a daze to the elevator where she rides alone to the lobby.

There are a few people coming and going, but it is still with quiet.

She holds her head high, her coat moist and teasing against

her bare skin. Her insides feel as though they've melted and the heat radiates outward, keeping her warm. She smiles at the man who holds the door for her, and when she steps out into the clear, crisp breeze, she looks straight up once again.

The sky is healed, the sun strong, screened by a bright blue sky.

The street hums and buzzes, people walking, talking, hurrying.

It is a beautiful day.

S IS FOR SENSUAL

"Come on, come on," Stephanie urged, grabbing hold of Camille's arm to tug her up next to her. Satisfied, she faced the door, threw her shoulders back, and rapped three times. Then she paused, rapped two more times, paused again, and gave another three raps. She grinned at Camille as if she'd just communicated with life on Mars. Her eyebrows wiggled in a "you're not going to believe what I just told them" sort of way.

Camille knew that look all too well. They'd been in Amsterdam a total of four days, and she'd seen and done more in those four days than she'd done the past four months. Her friends weren't letting anything pass them by, including time itself. But this, Camille looked around at the quaint little house nestled on a quaint little street. This place seemed a little too normal. In fact, if it weren't for the presence of the always wheeling and dealing Stephanie, Camille just might want to relax on that bench they'd just walked past in the lush, beautiful garden and have a strong cup of Dutch coffee with whoever lived here.

But Stephanie's wink sucked that little dream right out of her head. Something was going on. And why hadn't Crystal and Renee come along?

The doorknob clicked and turned and Stephanie bounced on the balls of her feet. Camille's heart rate accelerated a little as the door was pulled open to reveal a petite blonde with shoulder-length hair wearing a sleeveless white silk blouse and worn blue jeans. A quiet contradiction. Her smile was warm and friendly and her makeup was minimal. She waved them inside with soft hellos and welcomes.

Stephanie bounded in with a toothy grin and then turned to extend her arm toward Camille. "This is my very good friend, Camille," she said, as if Camille had not only landed on Mars but had actually flown the spacecraft herself after years of elite training, thus deeming her the best pilot on all of earth itself.

The woman eyed Camille quickly and gave her a soft but curious smile, extending her hand.

"Welcome. My name is Anna." Her accent was heavy but her voice light and pleasant. Her eyes were prettier than blue ice. Deeper.

Camille shook her hand and found it equally as warm and pleasantly firm. Nothing was worse than a limp handshake.

"Cammy. Call me Cammy, please," she stuttered. Anna only smiled, and Stephanie all but bounded right back out the door.

"I gotta go," she said, eyes suddenly fastened on her cell phone.

"What? Wait," Camille said, stepping to follow her. But Stephanie jerked her head up, shaking it.

"No. You stay here. I'll be back to get you in a few hours."

"A few hours?" Suddenly that beautiful garden just outside the front door seemed dangerous and alive, anxious to swallow up the house and all those inside. "What's going on?"

"Nothing." Stephanie grinned. "Just trust me, okay? You wait here. Anna will take good care of you." When Camille said nothing, Stephanie's grin faded. She looked serious, and serious for Stephanie was rare. "Come on, Cammy, you need this."

"Need what?"

"This." Stephanie almost whispered it. As if it were a secret and she didn't want Anna to know.

"What is *this* exactly?" Camille was more confused than ever and she was starting to feel more than a little anxious.

Stephanie sighed. "Just stay, okay? I'll be back in a while."

She held Camille's eyes a little longer and then exited, cell phone pressed to her ear, Nike Shox pressing on the stone path back through the garden.

Camille was about to chase her when Anna spoke.

"Is fine," she said softly, touching Camille on her forearm, forcing her mind back from Stephanie. Anna pushed the door closed and took her hand. "Come."

They headed left and into a roomy sitting area where two large chairs flanked the hearty stone fireplace. A hand-stitched pillow sat centered in each chair. One said "liefde" and the other said "ontwaken." She didn't know what either meant and she wished she had her pocket dictionary, but Stephanie had insisted that she bring nothing.

"Please sit," Anna instructed. Camille eased herself into one of the chairs and held the "wak" pillow in her lap. Anna disappeared around the corner into what Camille assumed to be the kitchen. She heard dishes clanking as she studied the room. The floor resembled the fireplace, only with larger, more flush stones. A red hand-stitched rug with an Indonesian influence sat in the center, accenting the related artwork and pieces on the nearby furniture.

On a colder day, Camille could easily imagine the room flickering with warm fire and smelling of freshly cut wood and apricot brandy. As if reading her mind, Anna returned carrying a thick glass. She handed it over carefully, as if it were valuable in ways Camille wasn't aware. It was chilled, and as Camille sipped she realized it was Coca-Cola and jenever. She'd tried the local spirit their first day in Amsterdam and she recognized it immediately.

It was strong, but Camille welcomed it, not realizing just how thirsty she was from their bike ride over, weaving through the maze of canals and tourists.

Anna watched her closely and encouraged another series of drinks by tipping the bottom of the glass with the pad of her index finger. It was a delicate gesture, deliberate and slow. As if Anna were offering her finger along with the drink. Camille obliged, taking a few more generous sips, but she cautioned herself, still feeling the effects of the half pints of beer she'd had earlier.

"You are hungry?" Anna asked.

"No, no, thanks. I had some uh, *patats* earlier. Those French fry things?"

Anna nodded and encouraged another drink.

When she was finished she held the glass out for Anna, who placed it on a nearby end table. Then she held her hand out for Camille. They stood and Camille followed her slowly to the steep staircase. They ascended slowly, the old wood creaking underfoot. Camille tried to imagine where they were headed, but she could come up with no answers. Her head swam with liquor and her body ached from days of bike riding and walking and sleeping in a cozy little hostel on a hard bed.

She knew she should be reserved and concerned about what she was doing there, but her current state of warm fuzziness and fatigue wouldn't allow it.

The floor creaked on the second level as well as they walked a short way to a bathroom. Anna flicked on the light and shoved a towel and washcloth into her arms.

"Now you bathe."

Camille stared at the simple sink, toilet, and small standing shower. "Excuse me?"

"Do it and do it quickly." Anna walked to the shower and turned on the water. Steam rose and floated to Camille.

She started to ask why, but Anna shoved a folded satin robe in her arms on top of the towel.

"Hurry. I explain later."

She left Camille dumbfounded, closing the door behind her. Camille stared a moment longer through the steam and then she disrobed and stepped into the hot water. It felt wonderful on her exhausted muscles and she could've stood there for days if not for Anna's instructions to hurry. So she soaped herself generously and washed her hair. After rinsing, she emerged, dried herself, and slipped into the robe. She folded her clothes and opened the door.

Anna was waiting. She took the clothes and tossed them down a laundry chute behind a small door in the wall of the bathroom. Then she took Camille's hand and led her across the hall to a large room facing the back of the house. Anna pushed open the door and encouraged Camille to enter. The room was plush with thick, deep maroon carpet, silk-covered walls, low lamplight, and various lush-looking lounges in shades of soft cream. It smelled of warm spice, just enough to comfort and not overwhelm. A very large screen partition covered the far right corner. Camille's gaze fell back to Anna, who moved to the antique bureau where she began lighting candles and arranging bottles of what appeared to be oil.

Then she moved to the one window and firmly closed the blinds. The room flickered in golds, as if alive and breathing. Camille stood in the center, turning and looking. Her brain dizzied and she rubbed her temple, overcome with the urge to lie down on one of the lounges and sink to a fast, heated sleep.

But in a flash it seemed Anna was back at her side, hand coasting lightly up and down Camille's arm. She touched her face and then trailed her hand down to her neck. Heat surged to the surface of Camille's skin, along with chill bumps. She was hot and cold at the same time. A contradiction. Just like Anna's blouse and jeans.

Anna smiled, as if she'd heard Camille's thoughts. She held Camille's face in her hands.

"Is okay." Her eyes were sparkling in the wavering light. Like light through a deep blue prism. She moved her hands lower, running them over the robe. Up and down, soothing her, so much so that Camille closed her eyes. Anna leaned in and placed a soft kiss on her cheek, then her neck, and then breathed in and out with warm breath.

"Is okay, Camille. You're okay." Her fingers went inside Camille's robe. Hot skin on skin and Camille breathed in deeply.

Her mind spun and her body surrendered, allowing Anna to slip the robe off her body.

They both stood still, inhaling and exhaling. Camille opened her eyes, felt her bare chest delight and then tighten under Anna's gaze. She tried to speak, but her lips were full and tingling. Anna's hands started again, running up and down, ever so lightly and then all over, firmer and quicker.

Camille shuddered and inhaled sharply. Her nerve endings were working despite her prominent buzz. She squeezed her legs together, a new sensation pulsing between them. Lust. Want. Desire.

Things she hadn't felt in so long. What was happening?

"There," Anna said. "You are beautiful. And you are ready." She took Camille's hand and led her to a lounge, one that was completely flat, and encouraged her to lie down.

The lounge seemed to embrace Camille as she lay back slowly. Anna stroked her face and Camille exhaled fully, falling into the imaginary arms of the lounge.

"Close your eyes," Anna whispered. "Good girl."

Camille willed her body to relax. She heard Anna move to the far right corner of the room and then, just as she was about to set to sea on her comfortably rocking boat, she heard the door open.

There was whispered movement, soft breathing, and then strokes to her face again. A warm body sat flush against her right leg, and when a new voice sounded, Camille opened her eyes.

"Hello, Camille."

The voice wasn't Anna's and neither was the face. Camille blinked, then blushed and tried to sit up.

"No, don't," the woman said gently, pressing Camille's shoulder. Her accent was different from Anna's, her voice deeper and more exotic, matching her eyes, which were a mesmerizing hazel. Light blue with a warm brown circle around the pupils. Like a marble, meeting but not melding.

"Call me Cammy," was the only thing she could think to say.

A grin lifted a corner of her mouth. "I like Camille." Her face was angular yet beautifully feminine with a strong jaw, straight Roman nose, and full but imperfect lips. A small dark freckle danced above them when she spoke, teasing.

Camille blushed again, this time feeling it all the way down to her bare chest. Her nipples contracted as if the air itself were pinching and tugging them upward.

The woman's eyes flicked over them and returned to Camille's face. The grin eased, but her eyes looked different, like someone had struck a match beneath the surface, lighting them.

"I am Maria," she said, her voice rich and assaulting, sprinkling over Camille's bare skin.

Camille tried to calm her breathing, to cool her heated skin, but nothing worked. Maria was sitting next to her, watching her, visually tasting and consuming her, setting her body afire without a single touch.

"You are not what I expected," Maria said, grinning again, showing Camille a row of white teeth. One tooth sat slightly over another and Camille found it beautiful and natural. She didn't like perfection when it came to beauty. She liked women. Real women.

"You expected me? I mean, I didn't even know where I was going, or even where I am."

Maria watched her closely and then ran a hand through her dark-as-midnight hair. It was sharply layered and rested just below her shoulders, showing off the elegant but strong column of her neck.

She stood, showing Camille that she was taller and more muscular than Anna, and walked to the bureau. She cinched the belt on her long satin sky blue robe and rifled through one of the top drawers for a cigarette. Bending, she lit it from the wick of a candle and inhaled sharply. When she exhaled, she spoke.

"I expected you to be smaller. Weak looking. Like a mouse."

Camille sat up and hugged herself. "I don't understand."

Maria crossed to the window and opened it. She smoked some more.

"You let your girlfriend of ten years sleep around on you. You knew and you did nothing."

Camille shook her head. "I—"

But Maria interrupted. "So you break up with her. Finally. But you aren't able to move on. Why is this?"

Heart pounding, Camille tried to think, to speak, to rationalize. "I can't stop thinking about her, about things."

"So go back to her," Maria said, waving a hand.

"I can't."

"Why not?"

"I don't trust her."

Maria pointed the cigarette at her. "Okay then." She took one last inhalation and then tossed it out the window. Then she closed the pane and walked to Camille.

She tilted her chin up and stared deep into her eyes.

"It is time to let go, then."

"How do you know so much?" Camille whispered.

"Because I'm the one who's going to fix it."

Camille swallowed, her throat tight with emotion and an anxious curiosity. "How?"

Maria's hand slid over the satin of her own robe to the belt. With a firm tug she loosened it and the robe slid from her shoulders and fell to her feet, revealing a black, shiny leather corset. Laces wove up the center leading to sheer covered breasts. Camille stared at her with lust and wonder. Her heart thumped loudly and she could feel it pounding in her neck.

"Like this," Maria said, gliding her hand along Camille's jaw, pulling her up to stand. Maria bent her head and parted her lips. The kiss was sudden and powerful, taking Camille completely by surprise.

Maria's lips were thick and warm, wet and smooth. They conquered quickly, taking and sucking Camille's as if they were starving for her and only her.

Maria tasted of the clove from her fragrant cigarette. Warm and spicy, like an embrace in the coldest and loneliest of worlds. Her scent was something different, something familiar like CK One. Musk, amber, rose, violet, and bergamot. Crisp and clean, yet tantalizing with a hint of masculinity.

Camille groaned softly and felt her knees go weak. Maria supported her, held her tight, and encouraged her with a thrust of her tongue. Camille responded with her own, surprising herself. They held fast, tongues swirling aggressively, Maria's hands grabbing her ass and back, squeezing as they moved up and down. A flash of heat and a flood of moisture shot between Camille's legs and she found herself aching and throbbing and trying to press against Maria's thigh.

But Maria's hand seemed to know this, gliding quickly down Camille's abdomen. When it reached her flesh, fingers slid into her folds, causing her to yelp with pleasure and shock. Maria stroked her quickly, all four fingers exploring, and then she pulled her hand away, along with her mouth.

She left Camille breathless and dizzy.

"You are ready," Maria said.

Camille swallowed and caught her breath. "Why do you both keep saying that?"

To her right Anna reappeared from behind the partition causing Camille to look twice. She wore a matching black corset, deep red lipstick, and her thick golden hair was swept back into a tight ponytail. Gone was her friendly smile. Her eyes still burned, but her jaw was set and her cheekbones sharply defined. Camille couldn't help but stare.

Anna met her gaze briefly but her expression did not change. She handed Maria a tasseled flogger and then returned to the partition. Camille watched as she pushed it together and moved it, exposing a tall black crucifix-looking object with extra arms and legs. She stared at it in confusion until Anna began adjusting the cuffs on each end.

Camille inhaled quickly and swayed. Maria's hand gently gripped her upper arm. She smiled. Camille shook her head and sat.

Maria stood over her.

"You are ready for this, Camille."

Camille said nothing; she kept looking back at the crucifix.

"Look at me," Maria said. "Camille, look at me."

Camille did so and she found her eyes sincere.

"This is not about that. This is about you. And me. And Anna."

"I don't understand."

Maria waited for Anna to return. When she did, they embraced and both of them looked at her.

"This is for you. We are here for you."

Camille didn't know what to say.

"Are you not attracted to us?" Maria asked.

Camille straightened. "Yes."

"Then forget the rest. Nothing else matters. All that matters is you and us and this room. Right now."

Maria held out her hand. Hesitantly, Camille took it and stood.

"Are you ready to let go?"

Camille burned with desire and burned with resentment for the past. She hated the way she felt, the way she'd felt for so long.

"Yes," she said before she dared change her mind.

"Do you trust me?" Maria asked. "I will not hurt you, Camille."

Camille swallowed, nodded, and said, "Yes."

Her heart tripled in rhythm.

"Good, now relax. I am going to mend you, body and soul. If at any time you want me to stop, say 'stop.' Any other word I will ignore."

"Okay," Camille breathed.

Maria turned to Anna and kissed her. It was a long, slow, deep kiss, one that showed slips of tongue almost right away. Camille watched in amazement as they kissed and sucked and thrust and kissed some more. Hungry tongues and ravenous lips, tugging, pulling, parting, and taking. Anna clung to Maria, arms around her neck. Maria lifted her by the buttocks, holding her firmly. Anna moaned, deeply but surrendering. She was ready, and suddenly Camille understood what that meant. Anna was ready, ready to let Maria take her. She could wait no longer, could take no more.

They parted and Anna was breathless. Maria held her with one arm and Anna gazed at her with beckoning surrender.

"Please," she was saying without speaking. "Take me."

Camille felt like a voyeur, but she was so turned on she couldn't bear to tear her eyes away. Maria looked at her, as if feeling the heat of her stare. She released Anna and took a step closer to Camille.

"Did you like that?" she asked.

Camille couldn't speak. Anna approached her as well. Maria's fingers tickled her arm. She leaned in and whispered, "I know you liked that." And her tongue snaked out to caress her ear

Chill bumps shot all over Camille's body. Her nipples gathered painfully and pointed upward, pleading to be touched. Their call was answered when Anna dipped her head and took the right one in her mouth. A hiss escaped Camille as the hot wet mouth closed over her and sucked, wet, slick tongue not far behind. It swirled along her bunched areola and flicked at her thick nipple. Without thinking, Camille's hand found the back of Anna's head where it clutched her ponytail and held her head in place.

Maria moved in further, kissing her mouth, her tongue swirling in the same motion as Anna's. Her left hand traced up and down Camille's hungry midsection, as if waiting for a dare to go lower. Up and down it went, winding Camille up with lust and desire.

Insanity almost overtook her as Anna briefly pulled away to lightly press her lips to Camille's cheek and neck. Maria pulled back as well and stared seriously into her eyes.

"It is time," she said.

Sparks and tingles danced beneath the skin of Camille's lips. Her breast felt tight and alive, craving the air, the flickering of the candles, anything and everything that could possibly touch it.

Anna took her hand and Camille noticed the new dullness of the lipstick. It made her lips look fuller and swollen, and there were traces of the red on Maria's lips and no doubt now on her own as well. The notion aroused her as if it were blood and they were three vampires feeding off one another.

She followed Anna slowly to the crucifix. The beating of her heart no longer alarmed her. Its quick rhythm was part of her now, a part of this. Whatever this was.

Anna guided her backward, pressing against the crucifix. It felt cool against her skin, and when her arms were spread outward she could tell it was covered in some sort of leather-like material. Fear, anxiousness, and excitement coursed through her as Anna tightened the cuffs along her wrists. More of it came when Anna stepped up and wrapped a satin blindfold around her head. She gave Camille a soft kiss just before she secured it over her eyes.

"Is okay," she said again.

Camille stood quivering inwardly. Her pulse raced along with her mind. But her body remained calm, limbs strong and sturdy, sex wet and needing. She breathed deeply and strained to hear.

She felt Anna nudge her legs apart and tighten the cuffs along her ankles. Then she heard Maria speak from a few feet in front of her.

"I want you to feel," she said. "I do not want you to see or to think. I want you to feel."

She heard more movement and then felt a tickle along her inner calf. Instinct told her to move her leg, but she couldn't. The tickle moved upward and then she felt another along her other leg.

"What is it?" she asked.

"Shh."

Camille clamped her mouth shut and the tickling spread to her inner thighs, causing more chill bumps to rise. The more the tickle touched her, the more familiar it seemed. And when it went up her body, circled her breasts, and touched her face, she knew it was a feather. Two feathers. Two very large feathers. But knowing what it was did nothing to quell the sensation. The feather continued on, tickling and stroking, along her arms to her fingertips and back up to her neck. Back down to her chest, around her breasts and down her stomach. At her pubis both feathers teased, mingling with her hair briefly before going around and down to her thighs once more.

It continued like this several more times until her body was straining for more touch. A light sweat had started along her brow, and she bit her lower lip in an effort for control.

"Do you want more?" Maria asked.

"Yes," she said quickly, the word tumbling out. At once, the feathers started again, this time rounding her breasts in a circling pattern, coming closer and closer to her nipples. Her muscles tightened and she thrust her chest forward. The feathers finally reached her and a soft cry came out of her and a shot of liquid-hot pleasure flooded between her legs. Over and around the feathers went, teasing and touching her exposed nipples. The lightest of caresses, of flickers, of strokes. Like the purposeful breath of Aphrodite upon the hungriest of skin.

She strained further, needing more, and the feathers went lower. They reached her sex and circled again, coming closer and closer. When they reached her they stroked her up and down, ever so lightly touching her bare flesh. The sensation caused her to tug harder in a spasm. Strange noises came from her throat.

"Please," she begged. "Please." She tried to spread herself open further, but she could not.

"Are you wanting more?" Maria asked.

She forced herself to swallow. "Yes. God, yes. Please."

There was silence and the feathering stopped. Her thudding pulse muffled any sound and then suddenly she felt fingers between her legs. Her back straightened and her head pressed back against the support. The fingers opened her and then she felt the feathers once again. Brushing over her, painting her flesh, driving her mad with want. She cried out, her voice rough and weak. Over and over her they went. One lightly caressing, the other pressing against her, painting her with her own arousal.

Then one feather rose back to her breasts, where it circled and circled again. Her hands fisted and her toes curled and Maria spoke softly to her.

"That is good, Camille. You are feeling now. Let yourself go."

Camille panted, clenched her eyes despite the blindfold. Her clit felt huge and hungry and she could imagine the tip of it reaching out for the feather. The touching wasn't near enough and she knew it wasn't meant to be. She tried to relax and ignore it, but it was impossible. She tried to relax and tolerate it, but that was equally impossible. Her body was a live wire, stripped and exposed. And the feather meant to tease.

Just at the moment when she was ready to scream and shake her head in an agony bordering on ecstasy, the fingers were gone along with the feather. A shudder overcame her, one of spent and still coiled energy. She could feel the cool sweat on her brow seeping into her hairline. Her own breathing sounded loud, adding a new instrument to the band consisting only of her drumming heart.

Nearby, she managed to hear what she thought were whispers. She strained to hear them, tugging on her cuffs and turning her head to the side. Movement stirred before her and she smelled Maria before she felt her.

"You ready for more?" Maria asked, leaning into Camille's ear and flicking the lobe with her tongue.

Camille nodded, unable to find her voice.

Fingers once again slipped inside her folds to explore. They did so expertly, gliding along the sides of her clit before barely dipping inside her hole.

"Yes, I'd say you're ready."

Maria kissed her roughly, tugging on her lips as her fingers squeezed together and tugged on her clit.

Camille groaned in that sweet agony once again and then Maria was gone. Camille blinked behind the blindfold, turning her head, listening.

More movement came before her and she felt a small pocket of heat close to her breast. She could feel Anna next to her, her breathing hitting Camille's upper shoulder. Then she felt what could only be Maria in front of her, kneeling down to her thighs. She felt hot breath on her inner thighs and then she felt a hot, slick tongue tracing upward.

She tensed and moaned and then she heard Maria say, "Do it."

A white-hot burning erupted down the middle of her chest, slamming her head back, opening her mouth, and just before she could scream, it was gone, numbed into a warmth she couldn't describe it.

"What—what was that?" she panted.

"It is you feeling," Maria said. "Like this." Her fingers spread Camille open.

Camille felt the tongue again, this time circling her clit. Just like the feather it went. Around and around, closer and closer.

And then Maria licked her dead-on. Hot, heavy tongue pressing and licking. Camille bucked despite the restraints. And then Maria stopped and said, "Again."

Camille braced herself and another hot, searing burn pierced her right breast. She cried out and then relaxed as the burn ceased and once again warmed and enveloped. The tongue followed suit, this time licking her dead-on right away.

"Oh fuck," Camille rasped as it pressed and licked and lapped and teased. "Oh fuck," she said again.

"Again," Maria called out, stopping only for a split second.

Camille braced herself, but she did not flinch. In fact, she found herself shoving her chest outward, eager. The burning came, this time on her left breast, and she cried out in ecstasy rather than pain. Maria kept licking, up and down and then side to side. She stopped only long enough to ask her if she liked it.

"Yes," Camille said. "Yes."

Maria rose then and kissed her full on, forcing her to taste herself. Then she shoved her fingers inside her and bit her neck. When she pulled back she said, "Yes, you do like it. But I think you need more."

The burning came again, this time all over her upper chest. The flames went down toward her midsection and then cooled within seconds. Maria's fingers plunged inward and upward as she demanded, "Again."

More fierce burning, this time down her belly. But she no longer cared. No longer felt the pain in a negative way. Instead she welcomed it and welcomed Maria.

"Let it go, Camille. And invite the pleasure."

"I am," she rasped.

"Are you?" The burning came again, on top of the encasing warmth.

"Yes—yes, I am." And she was. There was nothing in her mind but the present.

"Good," Maria purred. "You are very wet," she whispered. "But not wet enough."

She drew her fingers out slowly. Camille wanted to protest but fought against it. She felt Anna leave her side, along with Maria. When someone came back, she began picking at the warmth on her chest. Peeling it off carefully.

"What is that?" Camille asked.

"Wax," Anna said.

Camille strained like a giant exposed nerve as Anna cleaned the wax off her skin. With the warmth of the wax gone, her nipples contracted again and her body felt the cool air breathing against it.

Anna said nothing further as she finished and moved away. When she returned Camille could hear her squirting something from a bottle. Warm hands began spreading something slick along her body. Camille remembered the oil on the bureau and closed her eyes as Anna rubbed it all over her. When she reached her breasts she circled and then went over them lightly, squeezing the nipples between two fingers. Camille hissed and bucked her hips. Anna went lower, massaging the oil into her legs, down to her feet and between her toes. Then she rose and oiled her arms all the way to the fingertips. When she finished, she backed away and Camille stood pulsing in the silence.

Someone approached and she tensed, waiting.

And then it happened. Something hot spattered across her chest and stung. For an instant she thought Anna had returned and was once again throwing hot wax on her. But this sensation was different. It left her immediately and then burned again. There was a noise as well. A sort of whipping. And suddenly she remembered the flogger.

It came across her again, whipping her breasts. She made a noise of pain and once again found herself pushing her chest outward, hungry for more. That bittersweet agony came again and again. Snapping across her skin, pecking her nipples, slapping her areolas. Her noises grew stronger, louder. Begging then demanding.

More lashes came, and she imagined her skin brimming with redness, the blood seeking beneath and relishing under each strip of leather. The beat of her heart became the beating of her skin. Alive and wanting and needing.

She clenched her teeth as the switches went lower. She growled when they whipped across her sex. She flinched with every blow, small peeks of her flesh getting bitten by the straps. It was like flicking a terrible itch with your fingernail and then pulling away.

Nothing was enough.

As her thighs stung, she felt who she assumed to be Anna lowering herself between her legs. Hot breath was followed closely by eager fingers that spread her open once again. Then came the tongue. This one smaller but heavier. It flicked her clit as the whipping flicked her breasts.

She wanted to tear the arms off the crucifix, it felt so good. Painfully sweet lash after lash awakened her breasts while the thick velvet little tongue played with her clit. She groaned, head falling back, going from side to side. She pumped her hips as best she could, needing more pressure, needing that final push to send her into oblivion.

And then Maria called out, "Enough." And all stopped.

Camille went slack and hung from the binds. Her body was wound tight, but her mind couldn't take much more. Sweat now dripped from her temples and she was pretty sure it was beaded on her body as well.

Her heart tripled over itself as she struggled to calm herself. She thought about saying "stop," but she didn't want to give in. And she didn't want the pleasure to end.

The realization surprised her a bit. She'd never experimented sexually before, and she'd never imagined herself in a scenario even remotely close to this. Yet here she was and she was enjoying it.

There was movement in the room before her and she stood straight and tried to listen. To her surprise someone approached and removed the blindfold. It was Anna. She did not smile but she did touch her face and kiss her softly.

While Camille's eyes were still closed from the kiss, Anna moved to the restraints and loosened them. Camille opened her eyes and dropped her wrists. She immediately rubbed them as Anna loosened the ones around her ankles. When she was free,

Anna took her hand and led her to a lounge. This one had a long back and a side. She brought Camille to stand before it and then left her.

Camille waited quietly, but not for long.

"Are you ready to come, Camille?" Maria asked from behind.

Camille blinked away some sweat. "Yes." She did want to come. So badly she thought she might lose her mind. But she didn't know what was in store for her next, and the anticipation both frightened and excited her.

"Good," Maria purred, moving against her. Camille felt something wet and cool against her buttocks. Then she felt Maria's breath in her ear.

"Very good, Camille. It is time." She ran her hands along Camille's sides and down to her hips. Cupping them, she said. "Get on the couch on your hands and knees."

Camille did so carefully, liking the way the creamy soft material felt against her skin. With Anna's help, she crawled onto the lounge lengthwise so she was parallel with the long back. If she had wanted to she could've lain down. She felt Maria climb on behind her, and she readied herself as best she could for what was next.

There was a brief silence and then she felt the wet cool thing pressing into her opening, searching. When it found her completely, it surged inside her and she cried out and arched her back. Maria's hands found her hips once again and they clung to her, pulling her backward, fucking her harder.

"Oh God," Camille said, feeling the burn of the cock as it pushed against her walls and then tugged against them as it came back out. "Oh—oh, God," she said again as Maria drove into her, fucking her faster. The cock plunged into her heatedly again and again, burning and pressing and lunging and fucking. She was gripping it like a vise, squeezing it tightly as it went in and out. Her g-spot exploded into white-hot flames and the cock seemed to grow bigger and longer and hotter.

"Do you want to come?" Maria asked.

"Yes." Oh God, so bad. So bad.

"Let go, Camille. Let it all go."

"I—am," she breathed.

"Louder," Maria demanded, fucking her hot and deep and fast.

"I—am, I—oh God!" She came suddenly and her voice wasn't her own. It was lower, more primal, spawned from the deepest recesses of her being. Her back arched, head tilted, mouth open. Another series of flames shot down her back as Anna poured hot wax down her spinal crevice. Camille screamed in ecstasy and Maria kept fucking, forcing her hips back and forth.

"You want more?" Maria asked loudly while she was still coming.

"Ye—es."

Anna crawled on the lounge in front of Camille and lay down on her back underneath her. Then she slid backward so that Camille was staring down at her leather-covered crotch.

"Let her have you," Maria said.

Camille spread her knees wider and lowered her hips, and at once felt Anna's mouth beneath her. She braced herself with her arms and Maria continued to fuck her while Anna devoured her aching flesh.

"Oh—my—God," Camille said, squeezing her eyes shut. "Oh—fuck." The cock pummeled good and hard and Anna sucked her, taking her clit into her mouth and bobbing as if she were feeding.

"Oh—Jesus—fuck." Camille rocked. The pleasure intensified by the second and when she felt Anna's tongue slip over her encased clit she lost it and came again, this time so hard she pushed herself up and Maria grabbed and twisted her nipples from behind.

"Ohh—ahh!"

"That's it, my girl. Let it all out," Maria said.

"Oh God. Oh God."

Camille rode it out, smearing herself all over Anna's mouth for what seemed like hours, while behind her Maria kept forcing the cock in and out until she could obviously take no more.

Lungs desperate for air, Camille finally stilled and collapsed onto Anna, who was still fastened to her sex.

She lay still for a few moments and felt Maria pull out of her. Anna swirled her tongue and Camille jerked and lifted herself a little. Maria came back behind her and she knew they weren't finished.

"Do you want Anna now?" Maria asked.

Camille pushed up on her elbows and noticed the zipper lining Anna's crotch. As she said yes she tugged it down and found Anna's bare flesh waiting. Behind her, Maria breathed on her buttocks and encouraged her to lift them. Just as Camille's tongue hit Anna's flesh, Maria's mouth found hers. Camille groaned and spread Anna open further, suddenly ravenous. She found her flesh wet and tangy and she took her clit right away. Anna moaned and began speaking in a language Camille couldn't understand. She slithered beneath her and Camille groaned into her flesh as Maria's tongue flattened against her and moved.

All three began moaning and panting in unison. Mouths connected to flesh, smacking and licking. Anna continued to plea in a different language and Camille sucked and licked harder, shoving herself back into Maria's mouth.

When Anna began repeating herself, she knew she was close and she begged for more herself. "Now, oh God—please." And Maria licked her harder and faster, flicking the tip of her clit and then assaulting it fully with the heavy weight of her tongue.

Camille burst through the night a split second before Anna and they both cried out and rocked their hips. Camille licked her as long as she could before once again collapsing, thighs trembling. Beneath her Anna laughed, and she and Maria said something in the same foreign language. Camille wished she knew what they were saying, but as she rolled off Anna she realized she didn't care. She lay pressed against the length of the lounge as both women rose.

She found Maria watching her and she offered a small smile.

"She is not done," Maria said.

Anna, too, looked at her.

Maria took off the strap-on and handed it to Anna, who stepped into it and tightened it. Maria first wrapped her arms up and under Camille and tugged her legs down. Camille lay on her back, and she watched as Maria then came to sit behind her head. Anna went to the other end where she climbed on and spread Camille's legs. Anna entered her with the cock and held fast to her thighs. Camille closed her eyes and sighed, the burning fullness a complete and total welcome.

Anna began to pump her, slowly at first, but then she found a rhythm and pulled her harder, really fucking her good. Camille opened her eyes and moaned and above her she saw Maria straddling her face and easing herself down onto her.

Camille met her flesh with her tongue, and Maria rubbed herself against it, whispering words Camille couldn't make out. Camille lifted her arms around Maria's thighs and pulled her down. She sucked her clit and swirled over it with her tongue. Then she scooted back a bit and slid her tongue inside her. Maria called out and bucked her hips. Camille tongue-fucked her long and hard just as Anna fucked her below.

Maria rode her face, calling out frequently and urgently. Then she demanded. "Have you let it go, Camille?"

Camille moaned, her own orgasm approaching.

"Are you ready to move on?"

Again, Camille moaned.

"Say it!" Maria demanded.

Camille wretched her mouth away. "*Yes*!"

"Say it again!"

The cock continued, faster and faster.

"*Yes!*" she shouted.

"Good, now show me with your mouth!"

Camille found her flesh once again, sucked hungrily at the cool moisture dripping from it. Maria sucked in a quick breath, laughed deviously, and shoved herself onto her.

"Yes, that's it, Camille. Show me." She moved her hips in motion with Camille and she started to speak to Anna. "Give it to her. Give it to her now as I come."

Anna responded by slamming into her harder, grunting as she pulled on her thighs.

And then Maria came hard, rubbing herself in a frenzied spasm all over Camille's face. And before she stopped she threw herself down along Camille's body and fastened her mouth to Camille's flesh.

Camille shut her eyes again and came as Maria's tongue found her and Anna's cock filled her up so large and liquid hot. She came hard, crying out into oblivion, taking all that she could, never wanting it to stop, to end, to cease. She wanted to live in that very moment for all time. There, there, there where nothing mattered and nothing existed but pure floating pleasure.

She stayed there for a long while before she finally drifted downward. Her heart thudded in her head and between her legs. Maria rolled off her and sat next to her, stroking her face. Anna crawled between her legs to rest on her chest, cock still inside her.

They lay in silence, with Maria's soft strokes and Anna's heart beating against her own. The candlelight flickered and sang a silent song, and Camille's eyes fell closed and her body finally completely relaxed. She was in her boat now, swaying softly, and she fell back and rode it out to sea.

When she awoke she didn't know where she was. Sunlight slanted in through the bars of the blinds. She sat up and realized she was on a soft lounge asleep on a pillow under a blanket. She was nude.

On the bureau new candles sat in rows. And in the far corner the partition stood, hiding the crucifix. Camille ran a hand through her hair and stood.

She found her clothes on the bureau. Washed and neatly folded. She dressed quickly and headed down the stairs. The scent of fresh coffee met her halfway down. Anna met her at the entrance to the kitchen.

"You are up early." She had on a satin robe and offered Camille a hot mug.

Camille flushed at the sight of her, and everything they'd done the night before came rushing back. She held up a palm to the coffee. Anna took a sip and grinned a bit, that familiar sparkle in her deep ice eyes.

"You okay?"

Camille fought off another flush. "Yes." She breathed deeply and realized just how good she did feel. "I—yes. I feel really good." She smiled.

Anna returned it.

"Good."

Camille ran another hand through her hair. "Thank you." She wasn't sure if that was what she should say or not. "And tell Maria thanks too."

Anna grinned again. "No need. We enjoyed."

Camille headed for the door, her skin erupting in flames once again. When she reached it she pulled it open and found Stephanie getting ready to knock.

"Well, look at you," Stephanie said, slapping her on the shoulder.

Camille ducked outside, head lowered in embarrassment. She heard Stephanie speak to Anna for a brief moment as she headed toward the stone path. Stephanie soon joined her.

"Have a good night?" Her grin was shit eating, as always.

Camille hid a grin of her own. "Maybe."

"Maybe? I'd say so. You look like you ate way more than a canary."

"It was—good."

Stephanie laughed.

"Better than good," Camille added.

"That's what I'm talking about."

They reached their bicycles and as Camille was unlocking hers a wooden sign in the garden caught her eyes. It said "De Mender."

She stared at it for a long moment and then looked to Stephanie.

"Thanks," she said as Stephanie straddled her bike. Stephanie looked at her in surprise but then smiled.

"Don't mention it."

Camille boarded her bike and they set off down the road. As the wind played with her hair Camille thought back to the words on the sign. "De Mender."

The Mender.

H IS FOR HIGHER

The cheery ding of the elevator was nearly drowned out by the beat of her racing heart. The doors slid apart effortlessly, opening to a large viewing area and several beige carpeted hallways. She exited quickly and averted her gaze from the floor-to-ceiling windows on either side. She knew that beyond the thick black glass twinkled the millions of lights of Las Vegas, bright and colorful, beautiful and alluring. As hypnotizing as they were, they did little to ease her tummy-tumbling vertigo.

She was now atop one of the largest hotel casinos in Vegas, but she fisted her hands, trying not to think about it. Instead she focused on the promise she'd been made, and with that in mind she found her way to the correct room number and knocked. The door was answered almost immediately, and she was greeted with a silent but deadly smile.

Broderick was a beautiful butch, one of those women who went by their last names because their first names were too femme. Half Asian with dark olive skin, green glass eyes, and short dark hair, she stood about 5'6" and had toned arms with eager biceps that popped every time she moved them. Her tank top helped in that department this evening as she motioned for Eve to come inside.

"You're right on time," Broderick said, her tone rich with sinful intent. Eve stepped inside and returned the smile, her own intentions already seeped with sin themselves.

"I'm never late," she said, her gaze sweeping the large room. The lamp light was soft and low with the winking lights of the city as a backdrop. The sofa and two chairs were pushed to one side. And in the center sat an object about three feet high covered in a sheet. She could make out what looked like handlebars, and her stomach flipped with excitement.

"I hope for your sake you keep your promise," Eve said, wanting nothing less, as she crossed to the center of the room.

Broderick watched her, her eyes sparkling. "I never lie."

Eve grinned. "Good to know."

"Would you like a drink?"

"Not right now, thank you."

Broderick approached the object and ran her hand over the sheet lightly. She held Eve's gaze as she slowly circled it.

"I have only one rule," she said. "And that's that you remove your clothes before she removes hers."

Eve was amused by this and she agreed eagerly, starting with her soft T-shirt, lifting it over her head. Then she lowered the straps of her bra slowly, liking very much that Broderick was watching her hungrily. When she was free of the straps she unhooked the clasps and tossed the bra aside. Broderick licked her lips as Eve's nipples bunched and buoyed, exposed to the night air.

"You're stunning," Broderick said, her cheekbones crimsoning.

Eve merely smiled and started in on her khaki shorts. She pushed them down and off and then hooked her thumbs under the dark red panties she wore to match the bra. She was glad she did because Broderick seemed to like them. A lot.

When she was finished she stood waiting, hands lightly running over her skin. She was growing more excited by the second with Broderick visually devouring her and the object sitting and waiting between them.

"I don't think I've been this apprehensive in a long while," Eve said.

Broderick tore her gaze away from Eve's breasts to meet her eyes.

"Me neither." Her hands once again rested on the sheet, and when she looked at it she urged the sheet off, revealing her masterpiece one painful inch at a time before whipping the sheet off completely and allowing it to drift to the floor.

Eve felt her breath escape her as she took it in. The object became a machine and her mind hurried to understand it. The base was wide and strong looking with much needed girth. That led to what looked like a large saddle, well cushioned and covered in a shiny vinyl. Down the center of the seat there was a long hollow strip a few inches wide that she couldn't quite figure out. Handlebars came up off the front of it to support the rider, along with two low-hanging stirrups.

Broderick began moving around the room, looking in a stack of plastic storage drawers. Eve could see that Broderick kept things lined up and in order. Moving her hand from left to right, Broderick finally retrieved several small phallus-shaped objects and brought them to her.

"Pick your poison." She raised amused eyebrows. "They're for your anus. Don't worry. Everything is sterilized and I always use protection."

Eve blinked quickly at the sight and at the words, but she recovered just as quickly and chose. Broderick made a ticking noise with her mouth and returned the other two back in the drawer. Then she held a metal box in her hands and flipped a switch. The machine made a noise and Eve watched as a strip rose into the hollow of the saddle, showing off two screw ends. Most of the strip was covered in matching vinyl, and it meshed almost completely flush with the rest of the seat. Broderick took the anal probe and screwed it in place. Eve watched and could see that the metal strip had a tiny groove in it.

Broderick rose and went back to the drawers. This time she opened the middle one and brought more phallic objects to her. These were larger and clearly dildos and needed no explanation.

Eve chose and watched as Broderick screwed that one in place just ahead of the other. She went back to the metal box and moved a small joystick. The anal probe and the dildo moved along the groove, first farther apart and then closer together. She left them about three inches apart. Then she dug in her pockets, fished out two condoms, and slid them over the phalluses.

Then she messed again with the switches on the metal box.

Eve was surprised to see both the anal probe and dildo sink into the hollow, leaving the strip empty once again. Then they rose again halfway like secret rockets awaiting launch.

"Okay," Broderick said, setting the metal box on the stack of drawers. She rifled through the bottom drawer and came up with a palm full of tiny clamps with spongy ends. Holding out her hand, she again asked Eve to choose.

"For your clit," she said.

Eve chose and Broderick connected it to a long cord. Then she connected the remaining two clamps to two other cords. Whistling, she returned to the metal box and began powering everything up. Then she took Eve's hand and led her to the machine.

"Go ahead and climb on," she said, helping her slip a foot into the stirrup and swing her other leg over. "Insert the dildos carefully and make yourself comfortable." Eve eased down slowly, allowing the larger phallus to enter her an inch at a time. The condoms were lubricated so it made insertion a bit easier. Then she eased down her backside and her chest and throat tightened as the smaller phallus went into her anus.

"Good, now relax," Broderick said softly.

Eve exhaled long and slow and sank fully onto the seat. Broderick was studying her closely and she flipped a lever, causing the saddle to slide backward a bit while the base remained in place.

The saddle was even more comfortable than it appeared to be, with a well-cushioned bottom and sides. Eve was soon completely relaxed and ready for more. She gripped the handlebars and placed her other foot in the remaining stirrup and watched as Broderick adjusted the length for her. Then she grabbed the clamps and handed one to Eve.

"Place this on your clit."

Eve took it, noting the soft, spongy clips. Spreading herself with her free hand, she carefully placed the clamp along her clit and released it for closure. The pressure was strong but not painful. She felt herself swell, causing more pleasurable pressure.

"These are for your nipples," Broderick said, handing her the other two. Eve placed them on her nipples and released, and the same firm pressure squeezed her.

Her spine straightened as a rush of skin-tickling desire came over her.

Broderick took a long, slow look. Her eyes flickered with desire and the crimson on her cheeks plumed and grew. Eve could sense the elevated beating of her heart even from a few feet away.

"I'm all yours," Eve whispered, already imagining what all this machine was going to do for her.

Broderick seemed lost in her own world for a moment but then she blinked and walked to her metal box. Holding it in her hands, she looked at Eve and asked, "Are you ready for the best orgasm you've ever had?"

Eve licked her lips and revved the handlebars as if to accelerate, remembering their earlier conversation in the hotel bar. When it came to sex she had no limits. And she'd tried everything under the sun and behind the moon, searching for that ultimate orgasm, the one she'd never forget. The one that would take her as high as she could possibly go. Broderick had understood this, more so than the other attendees at the ultimate sex toy convention.

"I'm ready."

With a tilted grin Broderick flipped the first of numerous switches and Eve instantly felt the buzz on her nipples. Another chill swept over her as her breasts bunched and puckered. Then

Broderick hit another switch and more buzzing vibrated her clit. Eve gripped the handlebars and moved her hips, the buzzing intense.

"It's too much," she said, wanting to strip it off. But Broderick slowed the speed and Eve sighed and her back relaxed. She closed her eyes as the buzzing spread outward from her clit, sending pings of pleasure through her body. She moaned in deep delight and thought how very much she'd like to have one of these for home.

Broderick seemed to sense her growing pleasure and slowed it down even more. Eve opened her eyes in protest, but Broderick only smiled and fingered another switch. A deep groan escaped Eve's tightening throat as both the dildo and the anal probe were pushed into her fully. Her toes curled and her abdomen tightened. Strange cramps burned in the muscles just above her knees.

Broderick cooed to her, encouraging her to relax. She switched on another button, and this time vibrations reverberated throughout the entire saddle. Eve clung to the handlebars, and with every minuscule movement of the vibrations, both phalluses settled further in her.

She began to groan softly, in short, small grunts. To her surprise, the anal phallus began to please her before the dildo. The pressure and vibration of it stirred her in ways she had trouble describing. Deeper, it seemed, and more guttural and animalistic. Touching her and reaching her in a place that caused almost silly, childlike responses. It was pure pleasure in its most human, primitive form.

And then she felt the dildo as the seat began to slide back and forth. It impaled her with its fullness, hot and firm. Back and forth and back and forth. Her pussy tightened around it, held it secure, her wet tissue clinging and clamping. The vibrations hummed and buzzed through her and then came back down, her crotch the focal point. Her noises grew in length and in sound, in rhythm with the back-and-forth motion of the saddle.

Broderick watched with what could only be voyeuristic

delight. Her eyes glistened, her skin glowed, and she breathed sporadically with her lips full and parted. She held the metal box securely, her fingers moving as if deciphering Braille, her sight unnecessary.

With a quick inhalation, she flicked her finger, and the clamp on Eve's clitoris buzzed stronger, sending her into a mad frenzy of jerks and groans. Eyes closed tightly, she wrung the handlebars and flexed her legs in the stirrups.

Pleasurable heat pulsed from her clit, vagina, and anus. In powerful waves, in all shapes and sizes, forming from different sensations. Vibration, penetration, friction, pressure, fullness, and motion. All of it saturating her nerve endings relentlessly, rocketing to every inch of her body and drowning her brain in sugary, thick ecstasy.

She called out, control of her body darting away from her. "It's coming. It's coming fast." She squinted and bit her lower lip, trying desperately to slow the oncoming climax. This mesh of sensations was so good she wanted it to last. It was the evolution of pleasure, a great clay ball of all different colors, formed by hand. It was rolling through her now, so fast. So damn fast.

"Mmm, God. Ah God. It's coming."

"Just say the word and it's yours," Broderick said.

Eve struggled for breath, for words. Her mind worked hard, submerged in the liquid pleasure. She had it all now. Right now. Between her legs and pinching her nipples. There was only one thing missing.

She spoke. "I want you. I want you to feel it with me."

Broderick stood very still, her glistening eyes softening with thought. Her fingers finally moved, slowing first the clit clamp and then the vibration of her saddle. Eve's bones tingled, and she loosened her grip and fell limp into the rhythm of the back-and-forth sliding of the saddle.

Her heart stuttered along hurriedly in her chest and she breathed deeply to slow it. Broderick lowered the box and moved one of the large overstuffed chairs. She grunted as she pushed it into place right across from Eve. Then with eyes fastened to Eve, she began to slowly undress. She started with her tank top, slipping it off over her head. Her breasts were small with large, thick, dark nipples. They clustered as if caressed by the air. Next she lowered her jeans and tossed them aside, leaving her completely nude except for a pair of white Calvin Klein boxer briefs. Her hands eased into the sides and slid them down and off.

Eve swept over her with her gaze, loving how toned and muscular she was with strong, curved legs, abs that looked pinched in from the sides, and hard arms and shoulders.

"Yes," Eve said. "Yes."

Broderick bent and retrieved three more cords. She plugged them in quickly and dug in the plastic stack of drawers. Her back and shoulders flexed as she screwed on the chosen clamps. Her ass had the carved look of a sculpture, with a scooped indention in the side of each cheek. Her ass was paler than the rest of her.

With the clamps connected, Broderick moved back to the chair and sat, the cords sliding across the floor with her. Eve watched closely, swaying with the saddle, deftly controlling her breathing and her pleasure by slightly lifting herself in the stirrups each time it tried to build.

She found Broderick enticingly beautiful, and a rush of lust flooded her body when her host spread her legs over the thick armrests, exposing her dark, neatly trimmed center. Wetness reflected the low light and Eve licked her lips as Broderick opened herself further with her fingers and attached the clamp. Her abs tightened from the new pressure and she then attached the remaining two to her nipples. Again, her muscles tightened and her breasts flushed red and strained.

Broderick reached for the metal box that sat on a small table next to the chair. Dancing fingers set Eve alive again, first with the saddle vibrations and then with the clit and nipple buzzing. To her added delight the dildo began its movement as well, sliding up and down just a few inches every other second. She clenched her fingers, toes, and eyelids as the different sensations met and mingled and multiplied once again. Her body seemed to melt upon the seat, oozing around the phalluses. The burning of their fullness seared through her, into her ass, her belly, and into her heart, forcing it to double over in pounding. She rocked harder, urging the saddle on.

Broderick answered by anchoring the dildo in its full upward position and speeding up the back-and-forth motion of the saddle. Eve let out a deep, amorous laugh and she groaned when Broderick flicked her own switches, jerking as her own clamps came to life.

"Yes," Eve said again. "Feel it with me."

Broderick pressed her lips together and her eyes narrowed in pleasure, showing slits of lush lime green. The clamp buzzed on her clit, vibrating the surrounding wet pink flesh. A pool of arousal had already formed at her hole and Eve longed to penetrate her, imagined doing so with her tongue.

"Come with me, Broderick," Eve whispered, her voice ragged. "Please."

Broderick moaned and small whimpers began to come from her mouth. "Uh, uh, siiis, uh." The plume of red on her cheeks and on her breasts spread, meeting in the middle at her neck where her pulse was visibly sending. She arched her back and spread her legs further, pointing her toes. More sounds came, quicker and shorter. Her fingers flew over the switches, and she turned both Eve's and hers higher.

Eve cried out and laughed again. Giddy and hot and alive. She gripped the handlebars harder, pressed her body down further at the complete mercy of the saddle. Swimming in the hot tide of pleasure, she began to talk dirty, something she always did when she went out that deep, feet kicking at nothing but pleasure.

"Ah yeah. Ah, fuck yeah. Feels so good, baby. Feels so fucking good." Again the laughter, her head thrown back, an offering to the pleasure god. "I don't want it to stop. Fuck no. I love it. Love how good it makes me feel." She focused on Broderick, stared at the vibrating flesh between her legs. Looked deep into her now flaming eyes. Listened to her quick cries of ecstasy.

"Yes, baby. Don't make it stop. Ah God. It's the best. The best ever. The dick, the one in my ass, ah God, my clit. Fuck. Ah God. So good. It feels hot and full. It's fucking me. I'm riding it and it's fucking me. Do you feel it? Tell me you can feel it."

"I—can—I can feel it." Her fingers moved some and they both cried out as the buzzing reached an all-time high.

"Ahh, ah God yes!" Eve let out. She threw her head back again and groaned. "Yes, yes, yes. Give it to me. Give me the best one ever." She again looked to Broderick. "Did you hear me? Give me the best one ever."

Broderick stared at her, her eyes open but weighted with pleasure. "Here it is," she said, upping it one last time.

Eve called out to heaven above, screamed toward the ceiling as her clit burst into a million pieces of hot pleasure and soared into her body. Her legs kicked out, stirrups stretched. Walls of pleasure came. Big, thick, and warm, moving right through her, reaching into her bones along the way.

Then she heard Broderick cry out from the chair, her neck strained, her own mouth toward the ceiling. Eve stared at her wet, red flesh, at the movement of it, at the way her hips bucked off the cushion, demanding more.

And then Eve came again, this time the burning shot out from her vagina where it clung and squeezed down on the dildo. She shouted again and rocked on the saddle and then the buzzing on her clit collided with the dildo and she came a third time. And then, when she thought there couldn't be anything greater, a fourth climax came from deep inside her ass. She bucked and rocked and tried to call out, but her throat was full of bristles. Guttural groans and high, strained noises fell from her as she gripped and rode and fucked, her body bursting into an energy hotter than fire.

"This—is the—best—ev—er," she said, never wanting it to end. She rode on, melting further onto the seat, insisting on every last centimeter of pleasure. Broderick watched her, her own cries full of life. Eve closed her eyes, and as the last of the pleasure moved through her, she felt herself drift. Her body was liquid and heavy, but her mind and soul were light. She floated above herself, felt the pleasure in every last molecule of her being. So great that she only saw a bright white light. Nothing else existed. Only this energy. And the energy lasted a sweet fucking eternity.

"Oh God," she said, coming down. "Oh my fucking God." She meshed back into her flesh and opened her eyes. Broderick was silent and her fingers slowed things down. First the buzzing on the clit and then the vibrating of the saddle. Then she slowed the back-and-forth motion and retracted the phalluses a few inches. Sweat lined the dips in her abs and the dip in her collarbone. Her eyes shone.

Eve released the handlebars and flexed her sore fingers. She also removed her feet from the stirrups and noticed the redness along her soles. When she looked back at Broderick she was still breathless. She smiled.

"You were right," she managed, clearing her rough throat. "You didn't lie."

Broderick grinned and removed the clamp from her clit and her nipples. Carefully, she stood and walked to Eve and kissed her softly.

"No, I didn't. And I have another truth to tell you," she whispered.

"What's that?" Eve asked.

Broderick ran a smooth finger along Eve's arm. "It's even better the second time around."

A IS FOR ANIMAL

The deep Southern sun was high in the sky, warming the back of Catherine's neck, beading a light sweat along her brow. The barn before her was quiet, tall, and strong with faded red boards and an old tin roof. The door was closed but not completely, and it squeaked with the wind. In the near distance she could hear the chimes cling and clang from the front porch of the two story white clapboard house where the missus and the boss man lived. It sounded eerie yet comforting, reinforcing the fact that there was no one else around. The old Chevy had sputtered off a few minutes before, leaving a spiraling trail of dust behind it.

Forcing herself to swallow the rising lump in her throat, she pulled open the barn door and stepped inside. Closing it quickly, she stood in silence and willed her eyes to adjust to the darkness. Scent came before sight. Hay, moist earth and wood, manure, and gasoline. She loved the barn and sought refuge there often when she needed to lie down in the stiff hay and wink the world good-bye for a while. But it also was the place for something else. And every time she set foot inside it, her blood burned and pushed against her skin. She rubbed her arms nervously, her body already awakening. The smell of the barn and the sound of the disappearing sputtering truck was to her like the sound of a scraping bowl to a hungry dog.

She ran the back of her hand across her mouth, already tasting what it was she was after.

Light seeped in through the slats of wood, casting a yellow hue upon the bales of hay, some of them oozing into lazy piles toward the back center of the barn. To her immediate left sat one of the tractors, along with two push lawn mowers for the grass around the house, and one old Model T that no longer ran. Beyond them were a few stalls, one of them occupied with Ma Bella, the old cow. She could hear her scuffing in the distance.

Squinting, she tried to see further into the dim barn, more toward the right where sawhorses sat and tools hung from the walls. She saw her then. The missus. Standing alone and quiet, turned away from her, hands running lightly across the large thick wooden workbench.

Catherine walked further inside, heart beating madly.

"Is he…gone?" the missus asked.

"Yes."

Catherine took a few more steps, eyes trained on the missus's pale green housedress. Her long brown hair was pulled back into a tight bun and her feet were covered in simple sandals. She didn't turn to look at Catherine but rather kept staring at the table, running her elegant fingers across the grain of the wood.

"Are you all right?" Catherine asked. "Missus?"

"Don't call me that. I don't like it when you call me that." She looked at Catherine for the first time. Her eyes were chestnut brown and brimming with emotion. She looked back to her hands, her posture still perfect. "I know it's what he wants you to call us, that it's good Southern manners, but I don't like it."

"Okay."

And then she continued, her nerves showing by changing the subject. "I wasn't sure if he was gone. I was just in here checking on Ma and—"

Catherine could wait no longer. She stepped behind her, pressed her body against her, and inhaled the freshly scrubbed Ivory soap scent of her. "Helen," she whispered.

Helen responded at once, at first stiffening but then sighing and falling back into her arms.

"Catherine, please," she breathed.

Catherine closed her eyes as her hands found Helen's hips and her lips found the delicate flesh of her neck. Helen mumbled meekly and whispered, "Oh God."

Catherine's hands moved up, cupping and squeezing Helen's breasts. They were free and buoyant under the dress, just as they were every Wednesday afternoon.

Catherine massaged eagerly, her passion growing with every second. The hot blood came, rushing through Catherine, as if it would burst through her skin. Helen's skin seemed to heat too, and Catherine bit her then, hard and quick. Helen gasped and turned to her, kissing her full-on with firm, warm lips. She pulled away before Catherine had time to react, touching Catherine's face with trembling hands.

"You—I—I don't know what to do, how to stop this. I pray and I pray, yet all I think about is you." Her eyes searched Catherine's in desperation, her fingers quivering across Catherine's lips. "I love the sound of my name on your lips, the sound of you crying it out, oh God. Oh God, forgive me." Knotting her hands in Catherine's hair, she tugged her in for another kiss. Her lips searched Catherine's just as her eyes had. Seeking an answer Catherine knew she'd never find.

Why? What did it mean? But none of it mattered. It never mattered once they touched.

The heat Catherine had felt before came rushing back, boiling her blood, and she returned the kiss, sucking with her lips and probing with her tongue. Helen responded with a loud groan and she leaned completely into her as if her legs had turned to mush, anchoring her hands into her hair. The kiss turned more voracious, mouths pressed tightly together, lips parted wide, tongues swirling deeply.

That same something came over Catherine again, growing into that deep-seated, powerful need she experienced each time they were together. Like the insatiable drive of a predator after its prey. It was what she was meant to do. What her existence was all about. Instinctual and involuntary. Words she never truly understood until she touched Helen.

She had to have her, would kill to have her, would cross the deserts and swim the oceans, leap over mountains. She would do it all endlessly if she knew that Helen was waiting for her, somewhere, somehow. Her scent, her taste, the softness of her skin, the sound of her sighs, the vibration of her cries. She would die for it.

Hurriedly, Catherine lifted Helen off the ground by her buttocks. A short, high-pitched "ope" sound came from her, but Helen held tight and quickly wrapped her legs around Catherine as she was carried to the large hay pile in the back of the barn.

Boots scuffing along the floor, Catherine hurried as best she could, and when she reached the pile she headed straight into it to above her knees and collapsed upon her.

"Hurry," Helen pleaded.

Catherine held her face, felt the heat from her skin.

With a yearning so fierce she nearly cried, Catherine kissed her. The collision was hot and hungry, tongues darting and demanding right away. Teeth met teeth, the kissing so vehement and intense, their mouths devouring at a maddening pace. Catherine forced her weight on her fully, thrusting up to control the kiss, shoving her tongue in completely, conquering. Helen moaned and clung to her back, raking her nails down the thin cotton T-shirt. The burning tear of her skin urged Catherine on and she pressed her thigh between Helen's legs.

"Oh. Oh, Cath—" Helen murmured, turning her head away from the kiss. Catherine looked down at her with a gaze so hot she thought she'd burn her. Helen narrowed her eyes in heavy lust and moved her hands to Catherine's front where her fingers curled underneath the collar of the shirt. A quick splitting tear pierced the air as she ripped with all her strength. The shirt hung jaggedly to her lower abdomen, her tiny breasts puckering, keen for attention.

"You're so beautiful," Helen whispered, lowering her hands to tear the rest open. She pushed the shirt off Catherine's shoulders and tossed it aside. Then she fastened her mouth to Catherine's neck while her hands held and massaged the bare breasts.

The sensation was like being lost in the ice and snow and then coming upon the grandest, hottest fire that ever burned. Hands so soft they had to be an angel's. Mouth so hot and hungry it had to be the devil's. Both loved her and touched her and devoured her. She rocked in a heavy rhythm, caught up in a luscious purgatory. And then Helen moved her mouth lower to where her hands had been, taking in each breast for a long, generous kiss, sucking madly while sweeping her tongue graciously over her nipples.

Catherine cried out and pushed up on her arms, pelvis thrust down and onto Helen.

She arched powerfully, offering herself to Helen, loving the way she feasted and bestowed pleasure upon her aching breasts. Each hot, slippery caress traveled quickly to that spot between her legs and grew there, pulsing with the beat of her heart.

Catherine pressed into her a few moments longer and then she dropped and pinned Helen's arms by her side. Panting for breath, she lowered herself along Helen's body and released her arms to shove her dress up hurriedly. She found her bare legs and kissed them eagerly, gliding along her upper thighs to her center.

Helen gripped her hair and squeezed. She hissed as Catherine moved to her cotton panties, using her mouth to kiss through the moist fabric.

"God in heaven," Helen said, knotting her hair tighter and tighter. "Uh! Oh sweet God."

Catherine urged her tongue along the cotton, her face heating with wild desire. She could feel Helen's wetness, feel the firmness of the peaks and valleys of her collected flesh. She kissed her harder, knowing it was where she herself was dying to be touched. Where they both began and ended, their middle, their center. Their most sensitive, sensual place.

When she caught the hot, moist, tangy scent of her, Catherine growled and felt that elemental stirring raking across her insides. Having Helen in her mouth was her sole objective, her reason for breathing. She often imagined someone coming upon them as she fed, and she envisioned how she would tear her mouth away to bare her teeth at them and snarl as she swung her clawed hand. Like a beast protecting its kill. Helen was hers, if not for all of eternity, then for at least an hour every Wednesday afternoon. Nothing was going to take that away from her.

With frenzied hands, Catherine tugged down the panties, stripping them from around Helen's ankles. Dropping them upon the golden hay, she stared at Helen, mesmerized by the dancing dust particles sprinkling over her. A noise caught in her throat and her breathing came in quick rasps.

Helen's beauty was beyond anything Catherine had ever witnessed. Simple, slight, sweet. Yet complicated, emotional, and passionate.

She kissed and bit back up the pale legs, running her tongue over the light downy hairs on her upper thighs. Helen tensed, fingers intertwined into Catherine's hair, her own head held off the hay, watching her closely.

Catherine kept licking and kissing and nibbling, relishing in the scent of her, the feel of her, the quick tightening of her muscles beneath the skin. Her tongue hit the thicker hair and skimmed over the top of it, seeking the bare flesh. She found it in an instant and licked the length of it firmly.

"Uh, ah, sweet Jesus," Helen called out softly, gripping Catherine's head harder, holding her to her.

She licked again, up and down and up and down. Then she opened her further with gentle fingers and licked her some more. She paused between each lick, savoring the taste of her. Tangy sweet and heavy like honey. Enough was not fast coming, and she continued, focusing on the small cleft in the upper center. She licked it hard and firm at first and then quickened, flicking it from side to side, sending Helen into a small fit of jerky motions and unbelievable sounds.

She panted and begged and called Catherine's name. She trembled and shook and groaned deeply, head thrown back, neck arched and flexed, veins prominent like thick strings of thread. Her reactions were like the sweetest of music and the sound of dying prey. They lifted Catherine's soul and yet drove her to latch on and devour further. She took the elevated flesh into her mouth and sucked, using her tongue to thrust against the flesh with each tug inward. Helen reacted at once, nearly sitting up off the hay.

"Oh God, Catherine. Yes, oh God, yes."

And then she howled into the dancing dust particles and swayed back and forth, eyes shut and fingers clenched in Catherine's hair. A warm, slick rush of liquid pressed into Catherine's chin and she savored it, rubbing it along her face and lips as Helen's cries softened and silenced.

Loving the taste, Catherine ran her tongue along her own lips and swallowed. She flicked at the cleft once again and Helen yelped with sensitivity, pulling her up. Catherine crawled atop her.

Helen looked at her with wide eyes. She raised a quaking hand to her face. "God help me, I can't get enough of you."

Catherine knew that line all too well. Helen often fought internally over their affair, questioning herself and her devotion to her husband and God.

"I can't understand it or describe it," Helen said.

"Do you want me to stop?"

"No. I don't ever want you to stop."

"Do you want me inside you?"

There was a gasp and she closed her eyes. "Yes."

Helen readily spread her legs and Catherine lay on her side

next to her. Then, finding her slick hole easily, she thrust two fingers inside. Helen called out, not in words at first but in sound. And then, soon after, the words came.

"I can't control how bad I want you."

"Then don't try." Catherine went in harder and deeper, rocking her own body along with each thrust. Helen was wet but tight. So tight it almost hurt her fingers. It only drove her desire further. Beyond human need.

"It feels so right," Helen said, opening her eyes and gripping Catherine's arm. "Dear God, you feel so right."

Catherine kissed her, mouths open and pressed together, tongues and lips teasing. They breathed together, inhaling and exhaling each other's breath. When Helen moaned, Catherine took it in. When Helen tensed, Catherine fucked her harder.

"Please," Helen breathed. She fumbled hurriedly at Catherine's blue jeans, loosening them and shoving them down a bit. Catherine watched and waited with bated breath, and she almost screamed in rapture when Helen found her bare flesh.

Helen's eyes grew wide with wonder and then narrowed with desire. "You feel so good. So wet."

"It's what you do to me," Catherine rasped. Helen had never touched her there before and the control *she'd* tried to hold on to quickly rushed out of her body, forced by her racing blood.

"Oh God," Catherine whispered, climbing to her knees.

"Oh, yes, darling. Look at how beautiful you are." Helen watched her closely, her eyes searching, brimming with heat.

Catherine shoved into Helen harder, bending her fingers. Helen cried out and then bit her bottom lip as she too slid her fingers inside.

They both groaned in unison at the full, tight, burning sensation. And they fell into a quick rhythm, fucking each other with ardent fingers.

"Do you like it?" Helen asked.

"Yes."

"It feels so good," Helen said amidst more groans.
"Yes."

Catherine clenched her eyes and rocked. Then she opened them and stared into Helen's eyes.

"Watching you take pleasure…it's so different," Helen said. "I want to give it to you so badly. I would do anything to give it to you."

Catherine couldn't speak. She knew all too well.

"Oh, this is heaven, this is bliss, Catherine. Oh God, I can't take much more. Kiss me. Kiss me now."

Catherine bent and kissed her. Lips finding and taking right away, tongues adamant and demanding. With tightly squeezed fingers Catherine pummeled into her. She pumped as hard as she could and tensed as Helen did the same back. They grunted and groaned and sweated. Fucked like animals in the hay, madly giving and taking, allowing the raw desire for each other to overcome their minds and their bodies.

Catherine's small breasts swayed in the rhythm, puckering in the golden light. She wanted desperately to tear away the pale green dress, but she didn't dare. Just like she didn't dare to leave any marks along her neckline. This was their time and she needed their time like she needed air to breathe. She wouldn't do anything to risk that.

She bent again and took Helen's mouth with her own. They both came then, fingers fucking hard and firm and fast. They moaned into one another, eyes tightly closed, bodies tight, centers clenched.

Harder and harder Catherine went, rocking into her and pressing down on her. For an instant the hay felt and looked like a golden cloud. Way up high in the light of some distant sunset. Catherine could taste Helen's skin, feel it in her mouth, feel her wet muscle like walls around her fingers. She consumed it all, knowing she could never get enough.

And then she fell back down, rushing back to the barn floor, nestled in the hay. Their bodies stilled, save for heavy breathing. Catherine removed her fingers slowly and Helen sat up and did the same. The hay glowed in the sunlight and it smelled warmer and sweeter than before. Ma Bella mooed from her stall nearby.

Helen pulled on her panties and crawled to her knees. Her hands and eyes swept over Catherine's bare chest. Catherine inhaled sharply at the touch.

"Stand up," Helen said, her voice lower but thick with strength.

Catherine stood and reached for the waistband of her blue jeans. But Helen stopped her, grabbing her hands. She looked up at her from her knees. "I want you in my mouth."

In the far distance Catherine heard the old Chevy sputtering back down the road toward the house.

"No, he's coming back. He's early."

"I don't care." Helen held her hands and pressed her face into Catherine's open jeans. Her tongue found Catherine quickly where it began a hurried assault of her clitoris. Catherine jerked and hissed, but the truck sputtered closer.

"Helen, we can't. He—he's coming."

But Helen kept on, holding firm to Catherine's hands. She groaned into her flesh, whispered words of lust and desire. She flicked her tongue harder and heavier, begged Catherine to climax in her mouth.

"Let me have it, Catherine. I want it so badly," she said, looking up as her jaw worked and her tongue vibrated.

Heart pounding, flesh craving, Catherine gripped Helen's head and shoved herself against her. Helen moaned with further delight and Catherine swayed into her, loving the feel of her head bobbing between her legs. The climax hit just as the truck pulled next to the barn, engine sputtering loudly. Catherine cried out hoarsely, fucking Helen's mouth.

Helen extended her tongue and moved her head from side to side slowly, relishing every last bit.

"Oh God, Catherine." She smacked her lips. "You must let me do that again."

She stood and straightened her dress while Catherine hurriedly buttoned her jeans. Loose strands of brown hair fell clumsily along Helen's face. There was hay stuck in various places. Her lips were dark and swollen, her dress wrinkled. Outside, the truck engine died and the door squeaked open and closed. The boss man went toward the house, hollering for Helen.

"Meet me here again tonight," Helen whispered, still trying to smooth herself free of hay and wrinkles.

Catherine scooped up the remains of her shirt and held them in front of her chest. Luckily, her sack full of clothes was stashed in one of the empty stalls. But her attention went at once to Helen's request.

"It's too risky." She'd seen the boss man's temper and she wouldn't be the cause of him laying a hand on Helen.

"Then when? I can't wait until next Wednesday. I'll—I'll die."

Catherine touched her face and kissed her swollen lips. "I know." God, did she know.

The door to the house slammed and the boss man was walking toward the barn, still calling for Helen.

"You better go," Catherine whispered.

"I don't want to."

"Go."

"What's happening to me?" she called out, her voice soft but frightened.

Catherine moved away from her and hurried into Ma Bella's stall. She crouched there, back near her swatting tail as the barn door opened.

"I've been calling you," she heard the boss man say.

"Have you? I'm sorry. I was just busy with Ma Bella."

There was a brief silence. Then he spoke again.

"What's wrong with you? You look like a wild animal."

More silence. Then softly. "I am."

But the boss man didn't seem to hear it. Instead, he moved back out the door, saying, "I need my work boots and they're not in my truck."

Helen seemed to linger a moment and Catherine heard her say softly again, "I am."

N is for Never

I went to her that evening, when the entire sky was a pale yellow, fresh from a driving storm, set out to dry in the setting sun. She was sitting in her Adirondack chair, hair piled loosely upon her head, blue eyes flashing with contrariety. She was astonished to see me, yet knew at once why I was there. Thumb in her book to mark her place, she folded the corner of the page and set it aside. The words "What are you—" jumbled out of her just before I reached her. Quickly, I straddled her on the chair and watched as her eyes went wide with something that looked like fear and wonder mixed together. I took her face in my hands, and there in the cool damp setting of the sun, I dipped my head and kissed her.

Professor Susan Abbot lowered the page, hands and heart trembling. Her mind went back to five hours before when the very same words had caused a commotion in the roomy lecture hall. Whoops and whistles had rung out; a young man named Julio Garcia had stood and pumped his fist.

"Sit down, Mr. Garcia," she'd said, after clearing her tight throat.

After a long "what did I do" look, he sat with a defiant grin, high-fiving the young man next to him.

As the class quieted down, all eyes refocused on the lone figure standing in the back, holding her papers with long, elegant fingers.

Susan had spoken again, though barely able to. "Thank you, Tia."

"But I'm not finished." Her voice was as calm and as even as ever. Her aquamarine eyes focused on Susan as if there were no other person in the world, much less the roomy lecture hall.

"That's enough for now." Susan had been unable to handle hearing any more. And even now, in the quiet of her own home, she wondered just how much more she could take. She drew another long sip of her wine and curled her legs beneath her. She studied each word and ran her fingers over them as if they were raised and made of soft velour.

How could someone so young write the words that sang to her heart? It was impossible. Tia was only expressing her own feelings; it had nothing to do with her. And yet she couldn't help but wonder...

She rested her head against the chair and allowed her eyes to drift closed. Tia's face came to her. Pale like a cold winter sky with piercing blue green eyes. Thick dark lashes that fanned when she blinked. Her lips were the color of crushed pink velvet, a warm smile forever teasing at the corners. There was depth in her gaze, an ease in her movements, a calm in her soul.

Susan breathed deeply and her heart rate accelerated a little more as she imagined what it would be like to take those lips of crushed pink velvet into her mouth. Would they feel like the finest of satin, warmed by the rays of the sun?

She had asked herself that very same question five hours ago when her students had all hurried from the lecture hall and Tia had approached her desk to turn in the paper. Susan had been frazzled by her stare, knocking her own satchel off the edge of the desk, spilling papers and folders along the floor. She and Tia had both bent to retrieve them at the same time, knocking heads.

And as Susan had examined Tia, ensuring she was okay, her gaze had fallen upon those lips and the thoughts and late night fantasies had come suddenly and relentlessly. And in the next instant, in the complete acceptance and understanding she saw in Tia's eyes, tears had threatened to come.

She opened her eyes back to the present. As she reached for her wineglass, her eyes skimmed the framed picture illuminated by the lamplight.

Her heart leapt to her throat and then plummeted to her stomach. She winced. The pain was still so great. *Oh God.* Tears pooled in her eyes, not enough to run over, but just enough to sting. She gulped at the rest of the wine and rose to pad into the kitchen.

I'm not going to cry. I'm not going to cry.

When would the pain go away? Sometimes she felt so lost she found herself wandering about the house, aimless and numb.

She knuckled away the brimming tears and pulled the cork from the wine bottle. The dark liquid chugged into the glass and she took a sip quickly and then inhaled deeply. She made her way back to her chair and had just set her glass down when the doorbell rang. Straightening, she looked to the clock on the fireplace mantel.

It was after eight. And she wasn't expecting anyone.

The doorbell rang again and she crossed the room to the front door. She tried to peek through the side window, but she could see nothing. Thinking that it might be Dora from across the street searching for her cat, she opened the door.

To her great amazement, Tia stood looking back at her. Susan blinked, not quite sure if she was real.

"Hi." Tia smiled slightly.

"Uh, hello."

Tia had her hands in her coat pockets and she was rocking back on her heels as if to keep herself warm in the cold.

"Can I come in?" Her breath billowed out in small clouds.

Susan blinked again and Tia leaned forward a bit. "Please?" She fanned those eyelashes, and Susan saw the crescent-shaped mark below her eye where they had collided earlier in the day.

"Your eye, I'm so sorry." It had been dark red earlier. Now it had deepened to a blackish purple.

"It's okay, really. Can I please come in?"

Susan snapped awake from her dumbfounded trance and stepped back, swinging open the door. "Yes, please." The words sputtered out like water from a fussy spigot. Tia didn't seem to notice, though, sweeping a quick hand over her head to remove her knit cap. Her short dark hair framed her finely boned face in long, well-maneuvered layers. Short in the back and longer on top and on the sides, just over her ears. She unwound her scarf as Susan closed the door.

"Here, let me take those." Susan took the scarf and cap and waited as Tia slid out of her navy pea coat. Then she hung them next to her own on a shelf of coat hooks along the wall. When she turned back toward Tia she found her gazing around the room, one hand in her jeans pocket. Her cheeks were tinged from the cold, and she wore a tight-fitting gray thermal shirt.

"It suits you, you know?" Tia said.

Susan came to stand next to her. "What does?"

"Your house. All the wood and stained glass. Very arts 'n' crafts."

"Oh, yes, I guess it does. I really like it." The truth was that she'd spent years refurbishing it. It was her haven.

"You um, you sort of ran out on me today," Tia said, meeting her gaze.

Susan suddenly felt hot. "I'm sorry about that." They'd collided and Susan had focused on Tia's lips and then almost broken down in tears. She'd panicked and shoved everything into her satchel and then bolted from the room.

Tia smiled once again so easy and free that if the grin had fallen off her face, it would've been perfectly content surviving all on its own. "I didn't come for an apology."

Susan felt flustered all over again. Forcing her hands to remain at her sides, she walked into the sitting room and offered Tia a seat. Tia accepted and made a request.

"That wine looks good," she said, eyeing the glass. "If that's okay with you."

Susan hesitated a moment but then nodded and hurried into the kitchen. As she poured, she saw Tia bend and retrieve the papers from the chair. Eyeing them, she walked into the kitchen. She had found her own paper.

"So what did you think?"

Susan blushed profusely and stared at the wine bottle, wishing she could jump inside and hide. *How does she do this to me?* She cleared her throat and forced herself to sound calm, almost lighthearted.

"It's good. It's very good."

Tia ran her eyes over it and moved her lips in silence. Then she looked up and Susan could almost see the Caribbean sea of her eyes swell with waves. Something profound was about to come from her lips.

"I wrote—I mean, I wrote it—"

Oh God, she's going to say it. She's going to say she wrote it for me.

But Tia faltered and let her words hang and eventually fall. Obviously rattled, she dug in her back pocket and produced a cream-colored envelope.

"I've been meaning to give this to you. I was going to do it today, but you left in such a hurry."

She held it out for Susan, who handed over the wine. Tia sipped heartily and Susan couldn't help but watch as it darkened the pale pink of her lips. Blushing again, she focused on the envelope and noted that it was shaped like a greeting card. She slid open the seal and pulled out a soft pastel-colored card. As she read, her breath caught and tears filled her eyes. Her hands shook as she lowered the card. Tia watched her closely, blinking her lashes very slowly.

"Thank you," Susan whispered.

"I wanted you to know how sorry I am. Fitz was really special, and I know how hard it must be for you."

Susan wiped away spilling tears. "Yes, it hasn't been easy."

"He was something," Tia said softly, sipping more of her wine.

Susan wiped away more tears and moved back into the sitting room. Tia followed and eased herself into the neighboring chair and watched as Susan perched on her own.

"There's another reason I came," Tia said, eyes flashing in the lamplight. She held her glass carefully and Susan stared at the thick silver ring on her middle finger.

"Oh?"

Tia took another long sip and set her glass aside. Then she rose and crossed to the entryway to dig in her coat. She slipped her hand inside the pocket and retrieved what looked like a small book.

Susan drank more wine as she waited.

Tia approached cautiously, her eyes intense and almost... shy.

"What is it?" Susan asked, wondering what could've come over her so suddenly. But then her gaze fell on the book in Tia's hand.

Susan stood, alarmed. Her heart sank to her feet and then went wild like a jackhammer behind her ribs.

"It must've fallen out of your bag," Tia said softly.

Susan stepped backward, her feet searching for safe ground. Tia kept coming, book held out, eyes penetrating Susan's soul.

"You left and it was lying open just under the desk. I wasn't sure what it was at first, so I—I read." She stopped her forward motion and stared. Her delicate face had fallen a bit and her neck was patched with red as if she were nervous. She licked her lips quickly. "I'm sorry. Had I known what it was, I wouldn't have…"

Susan braced herself with a hand against the wall. Her sitting room spun. Tia placed the journal on the end table and wiped her palms on her jeans. For the first time since Susan had laid eyes on her, the young woman seemed embarrassed and unsure. She stood looking at Susan in an uncertain way. Staring into her eyes and then looking away quickly.

Susan wanted to run, to retreat to her bedroom and close the world out. Her haven no longer was the keeper of her most intimate thoughts. The outside had crept in. How could this have happened? She swore never to let it happen. And yet it had. In the haste and confusion of morning madness, she must've put the journal into her satchel along with a stack of graded papers. She inwardly cursed herself for her carelessness.

Susan's breath hitched again as the panic and reality of the situation crawled over her body like a hungry vine. She covered her mouth with her hand and fought off sobbing. She couldn't speak; she had no idea what to say or if she was even able to form words at all. Embarrassment, shame, grief, and the horrible feeling of being exposed, it all bombarded her mind.

Tia held her gaze. Then she ran a nervous hand through her hair and took a couple of steps forward. But then she stopped, took another step, and then retracted. Taking a long, deep breath, she stepped forward again, and in a rush of fluid movement she said, "I'll go, but first I have to do this."

And then she was reaching to cup Susan's jaw with her right hand. Susan saw the velvet petal lips, the clear intensity of her eyes, the delicate shutter of her lashes. And then, like a soft breath, she felt her.

There was a slight heat, clement like, a gentle, tender giving of wet, thick silk. Susan fell into it at once, her knees nearly crumbling. A sound like a sigh to God escaped from her, and Tia pressed further, giving more of her lips, offering Susan a gift beyond her wildest imagination.

And suddenly, it hit her.

Tia knew.

The journal was full of Susan's thoughts and feelings regarding Tia's words and her mind and her body. *Oh God, she knows. Oh God, she can kiss.* Susan's world was spinning faster and unraveling even quicker.

"Wait, no, I—"

Tia stopped and pulled away. She searched Susan's eyes.

"This. Can't. Happen," Susan said, hating every word.

"Why not?" Tia asked softly, kissing her lightly and then pulling away again.

Susan pushed on her shoulders in a helpless attempt to hold her at bay. "Because you're my student."

Tia wasn't fazed. "For two more weeks." She grazed her thumb along Susan's cheek. "And I already have a ninety-eight percent and my final paper finished."

Susan struggled to find more reasons. There had to be more. "You're so young, I couldn't possibly—"

"I'm twenty-four."

"Oh? I thought you were much younger—"

"You're running out of reasons."

Susan closed her mouth and came up with one more.

"I swore I would never get involved with a student." There, that would do it. Her career-long declaration.

But Tia only grinned. "Never say never."

Susan stared in disbelief. The jackhammering of her heart started again. Tia moved in closer, her eyes fastened to Susan's mouth.

"I'm going to kiss you again," she whispered.

Susan let out a soft cry, a whimper of desperation.

"Hurry." The word came out on a hush, shocking them both. Tia responded by pushing into her and breathing along her neck. Susan's skin came alive and she could imagine millions of tiny hands reaching out, desperate for Tia's touch. Tia moved slowly, breathing upon her shoulder, up to her neck, over to Susan's jawline. When she reached her lips, Susan watched as Tia's eyes fell shut and her head tilted. Susan then closed her own eyes and welcomed the kiss.

Heavy, slick lips connected with hers, opening and closing. Susan kissed her back tentatively at first, tugging slightly. Tia moaned and her tongue reached out, hot and slick, begging for permission to enter. The feel of it sent shock waves of lust down her spine and she stiffened, clutching Tia's short hair.

"Wait," she breathed. She still wasn't sure. Wait, yes, she was.

Tia held Susan's face. She stared hard into her eyes, her breathing rapid. She swallowed, licked her lips hurriedly, and said, "If you're going to tell me no, then tell me now. Because if you don't and we continue, I'm telling you right now, I might not be able to stop."

Susan inhaled a shaky breath, lost in her eyes.

"It would kill me," Tia whispered.

"Okay," she breathed.

"Yes?"

"Yes."

"Oh, thank God." Tia pressed into her again and this time Susan wrapped her arms around her shoulders and held tight. Her hot tongue came, and Susan took it eagerly, sucking it into her mouth and then using her own to explore in return. Over and over they kissed, Tia's mouth so sultry and sugary.

Soon that sweet mouth was on Susan's neck and Susan held on to her tightly, gasping in sheer surprise and pleasure each time Tia bit and sucked.

"Take me to your bedroom," Tia said, breathing into her ear. Gooseflesh erupted all over Susan's body and she dug her nails into Tia's back.

Getting a brief control over herself she said, "This way," and took her hand. She led them down the short hallway and into her room. She stood before the bed in the gray light. Tia looked around at the queen-sized bed and dresser. Then she went to the wall and flipped on the light. Susan hugged herself as if it had caressed her.

"I want to be able to see you."

Susan swallowed. *I want to see you too.*

Tia stripped off her shirt and flexed her jaw. Her small breasts contracted, the rouge nipples thick and firm. Susan caught her breath at the sight.

Tia ran her hands over her own body, exciting her crinkled breasts even more.

"I've thought of you, Susan. So many times. The words I've written, they were written for you. About you. Did you know that? Yes, I think you knew." She drew her hand down to her jeans and unbuttoned all the way down the fly. She wore no panties. "Here." She took Susan's hand and pushed it into her pants. "I want you to feel what you do to me."

Susan gasped first, feeling Tia's bare skin beneath her hand. When she reached the slick gathering of flesh, she gasped again and Tia jerked and narrowed her eyes with desire.

"Yes," she hissed. "Feel me."

"I feel you," Susan whispered.

"You feel how wet I am."

Susan dipped her fingers in the slick arousal and massaged her. "Yes."

"Do you know that's because of you?" Her eyes were nearly closed, her pulse jumping in her neck.

"Yes."

"Ssst, ah, ah, yes. What you do to me, Susan. I want to feel you." Hurriedly, she slipped Susan's sweater off over her head. Then she ran her palms over the front of her bra and unhooked the clasp between her breasts. Her eyes grew wide as the bra slid from Susan's shoulders.

The night air and light caressed Susan for real this time, and her breasts responded by tightening. Tia dipped her head and took one in her mouth. Susan arched into her, massaging Tia's breasts in return. Then Tia moved her hands lower and straightened. She undid Susan's jeans, allowing her flattened hand to glide inside.

A short cry came from Susan as the long fingers hit her flesh. She clung to Tia for support and squeezed her eyes shut.

"Ah, yes, so wet." Tia leaned in and whispered in her ear. "I have dreamt of this moment. And I know you have too."

Susan moaned and returned her hand to Tia's bare flesh and they rubbed and slid over each other together, hands down one another's pants.

Tia kissed her and flicked and teased with her tongue. Susan did the same and their tongues played just as their fingers did, to the point where they could no longer stand.

Tia kicked off her shoes and they shed their jeans. Susan stripped off her panties and they both removed their socks. They stood looking at one another in the lamplight. Their eyes burning trails all over their bare skin.

"You are beyond beautiful," Susan said. She could've never accurately imagined Tia like this. The creamy flawlessness of her skin, the curve of her hips, the tight, deep pink of her areolas. When she moved, the muscles in her legs showed, and Susan couldn't seem to tear her eyes away. "You're like a dancer," she whispered.

"I am a dancer," she said, coming in for another kiss. Carefully, she eased Susan back onto the bed. They slid up and stripped back the covers. Tia lay on top of her and maneuvered the sheet around her waist. She straddled Susan's thigh and moved back and forth.

Susan watched in amazement as Tia's upper body moved in the low light. She could feel the slick heat of her flesh on her leg.

"This feels so good," Tia said. "Feeling you beneath me." She bent for a kiss and seared her tongue into Susan's mouth. Then she sat back up and eased her hand along Susan's thigh to her center. She teased her flesh with her fingers and then shot inside her.

Susan strained upward and groaned, the fingers pushing through every cell in her body. "Tia," she said.

"I'm right here."

"Tia," she said again, and Tia bent and kissed her, pressing her back against the bed.

"I feel you," she said between passionate, long, pulling kisses. "Feel me inside you." She began to pump her fingers. "Come with me inside you." She fastened to her neck, surging into her. "Come, Susan. Come for me."

Susan groaned in ecstasy and her body flexed and tightened. She ran her nails down Tia's back.

Tia devoured her with her mouth, rubbing her nude body all over Susan's. She smelled of plumeria and rich shampoo. And she was there in her bed and in her body. Loving her, taking her, giving to her.

"Ah God, you feel so good," Tia said.

Susan held her tight and closed her eyes as the pleasure mounted. Tia seemed to sense it and she pressed into her harder.

"Come, baby, that's it. Come."

It came and it came, closer and closer as if responding to every word. Susan clung tighter, closed her eyes, and then it hit her, and she strained and cried out and Tia bit her neck and twirled her tongue in her ear and said that she loved her. She loved her and she was beautiful and she was everything and, yes, baby, take it, take all of me.

And then it was gone, just as quickly as it had come. It left Susan lying there, hands still pressed into Tia's back. She held her close and inhaled her neck and hair. She felt her heartbeat and heard every breath.

Tia laughed softly in her ear and sat up. She started to move again.

"Give me your hands," she said gently.

Susan did and Tia clung to them as she rode against her thigh. Susan locked her arms and watched as she quickened her hips and slid over her own arousal. Her eyes gleamed like tinder and she moaned in delight.

"I'm coming now, Susan. Oh, Susan, here I come. Oh, oh God." Faster and faster she moved, her hips on autopilot, whipping and jerking back and forth. Hot, slick wetness ran down Susan's thigh, and Tia pushed harder and then she said, "Here I—" and she cried out and arched her back and shouted to the ceiling. She rocked and rocked and she said *I love you* again and Susan told her the same and watched in sheer wonder as she slowed and then stopped and then collapsed upon her once again.

"I love you," Susan whispered, knowing she'd never seen anyone so thoroughly beautiful, inside and out.

"I know," Tia said softly. "I read every word."

Susan warmed and blushed. She tugged her closer. "I did too."

D IS FOR DARING

"Name?"

My face flushed with heat. She wanted my name, my credit card, my identity. I wished for the hundredth time that I could do this from the privacy and safety of my office. But it was too risky. The computer wanted everything the flower girl currently did. The only difference was that the flower girl accepted my anonymity just as readily as she accepted my cold hard cash.

She had probably seen dozens like me. Nervous, fidgety, anonymous. Many of us probably adulterers, playing Russian roulette with our intimate lives.

"The receiver's name is Cartwright," I finally managed, the guilt starting to eat away at me like hundreds of tiny morally starved piranhas. "Emily Cartwright."

I'm not an adulterer. I'm not married...but Emily is.

The name burned through me and caused my cool hidden blood to heat and pound with a purpose, showing itself just beneath my skin. I glanced around anxiously, half expecting bloodthirsty husbands to come crawling out from the walls, dying to puncture my veins and suck the life from me. *Fuck.*

The girl and her eyebrow pegged me as if she knew every detail of my situation and she strongly disapproved. I nearly melted on the spot, my body was so hot and alive with infatuation and fear. Infatuation for a woman I barely knew and fear of the consequences of getting caught.

"Address?"

Emily's home address flashed through my head. I knew it by heart. Knew everything there was to know about her by heart.

No. Can't do it. Too risky.

"Two thirteen Willow Avenue. Suite one hundred."

Cartwright and Associates, to be exact. The place where I made my living.

"Three dozen long-stemmed roses. Red. The darkest red we have." She repeated my specific order and then waited for me to nod. "I'll send them out right away."

I drove back to the office, anxious and nearly dizzy with the anticipation. The two previous times I'd ordered her roses I'd been too chicken shit to watch her receive them. Today, however, I couldn't stand the thought of not knowing.

Panic crept up my spine at the thought of my actions making Emily uncomfortable. Even though I had made it clear in my very first letter to her that it wasn't my intention to be intrusive in any way, it still worried me. It was my biggest fear, next to being exposed.

I wanted her to feel special, beautiful, respected, appreciated.

From the comfort of anonymity, I could voice all these things. What I felt, thought, wanted. I was safe here. In complete control. There was no rejection, no expectations, no hurt. It was just me, romancing a woman with all my heart and soul, without risking my heart and soul.

I'd done nothing but think of her for a year straight before I acted on my desires. My thoughts drifted back to when it had all begun. Val, one of the other partners, had come to a screeching halt outside my door one afternoon. She was breathless, her eyes wide.

"It's Emily," was all she said.

We ran down the hallway, and I heard the commotion before I saw it. Glass breaking, wood splintering. Her office door was ajar, and Emily stood in silence, gripping the remnants of a broken picture frame. Her chest rose and fell quickly and she spoke without looking, knowing we were there.

"I'm fine." But her voice was trembling. After a moment of silence, she brought her pained eyes up to meet ours. They were piercing gray and so full of pain it reminded me of a thunderhead ready to burst with a summer storm. When she spoke again, I almost readied myself for the crack of thunder. But she surprised me with her simple statement. "I'm filing for divorce."

It was all she needed to say. I understood, and what I didn't know, Val soon clued me in on. Jack had been caught with his hand in the cookie jar, their finances were in ruins, and Emily wanted out. Jack, though, didn't seem to want to let go.

I couldn't blame him. I wouldn't want to give Emily up either. And thus began my mad attempt to woo her from afar. I felt she needed me, needed my words, my thoughts, my feelings.

I only hoped I was right.

I held onto that thought as I entered Cartwright and Associates. The office was quiet and my secretary Prairie was probably outside enjoying a smoke. I sank down into the leather chair behind my desk. Thinking about Emily always put me in a trance, and I drifted comfortably in that warm place where only she and I existed.

My mind heavy with the thought of her, I began writing down random thoughts with a pencil. Bits of the next letter or poem.

My hand worked furiously as the images came. Emily had become everything to me. I would sacrifice anything, everything to see her happy, see her smile, see her feel the love that I had for her.

If she only knew.

But ultimately, she couldn't know.

A figure stepped into the doorway and I glanced up, expecting to see Prairie and her hair-sprayed helmet of bottle-platinum hair. I nearly choked when I caught sight of the woman staring me down with her cool gray eyes. Emily gave a slight smile, and my system struggled to adjust to seeing her for the first time that day. She stood all confidence and carved beauty, a shoulder leaning casually on the luckiest fucking doorjamb on the planet. One would never know by her presence that she was hurting deep inside. She was a strong woman. Brave and breathtaking.

"Am I interrupting?"

Oh God, yes. Every single time you step into my world.

"No, of course not."

She took a step in and my eyes couldn't help but travel up and down her tailored slacks and fitted blouse. I immediately envisioned what I always thought she would wear underneath. What I had written down on the piece of paper under my hand.

Emily,
Red.
Lace.
Rich like velvet.
Dark and smooth and satin.
Teasingly covering her creamy skin in seductive webs of deep ruby.
My lips sucking through the satin lingerie.
Her neck, arching and showing itself, paling from the moonlight as her head tilts back
Her hair, cascading over her shoulders like ocean waves inked by night.
Red.
Clinging to her skin.
Dark and moist from my mouth.
Red.

"I was wondering if you were working on the Meyer file?"

My brain screamed back from my world of ripe, racy red.

"No." I blinked a few times too fast, afraid that she would be able to see the secret thoughts in my eyes. "I don't think so."

You don't think so?

Emily seemed to consider my response curiously and uncrossed her arms as she approached. My breathing began to coincide with her steps, leaving my body in bursts as she inched closer. She rested a graceful hand on one of the two smaller chairs facing my desk. Her perfume collided with the air I was having trouble holding in. My pupils threatened to dilate at her scent. She was my drug. And I was dangerously addicted.

"You *were* working on it, weren't you?" She glanced over my desk, and I hastily covered the paper I had been writing on with my hands. Her gaze lingered over the very obvious culprits and I lifted one hurriedly to scratch my face in hopes of appearing more at ease. She took her time meeting my eyes, and when she did the slight grin grew, nailing me to my chair.

I struggled to breathe, completely pinned by her presence and the silent words her eyes were whispering.

I know you're up to something. I know it's you.

"Brynn?"

My body jerked. "I'm sorry?"

"The Meyer file?"

"Right." I skimmed my desk frantically, having lost all rational thought. "I'm not sure where it is…" I rifled through papers and in my panic brushed the one with my thoughts of her off the surface. It drifted slowly through the air, like a feather finally free of the bird. It fell to rest on the floor at my feet. I didn't budge. I didn't breathe. I couldn't breathe. I hoped that she would ignore it. I knew she couldn't read it from where she stood.

"Aren't you going to get that?" Her eyes were trained on the sacred piece of parchment.

To my astonishment, I let out a laugh. "That? Oh no, it's nothing. Just a piece of paper."

You're a fucking moron and she knows you're a fucking moron. Look at her. She's looking at you like you're a fucking moron.

"The file…" I stuttered, my mind suddenly functioning. I'd do anything to get her to stop looking at me. "I finished with it yesterday. Billy should have it." I sat frozen with fear in my chair. She was the predator and I was the prey. If I didn't move, maybe she wouldn't see me. I certainly was turning the same color as my chair. Burgundy.

Her hypnotic eyes were passionate and penetrating, the kind that offered little detail but unbelievably great depth.

"Okay then," she finally spoke, her voice soft yet husky. "I guess I need to find Billy." She smiled, her expression completely platonic, glanced down at the paper one last time, and then walked from my office.

I sat in the vacuum of her absence trying desperately to calm my flying heart rate. I closed my eyes and counted to five.

One. Breathe, Brynn, breathe.
Two. Christ, I can still smell her.
Three. You're a moron. A fucking moron.
Four. Her eyes, her body, her piercing eyes.
Five. I'm doomed. Completely doomed.

I walked to the door and pushed it closed. Pressed my face against its cool surface as my lungs filled with grateful air. It was getting worse, this addiction of mine.

I squeezed my eyes closed in shame and frustration. She was still there, in my mind's eye. Grinning at me. In red. Red like the roses I give to her.

A knock in my ear caused me to jump.

"You have the Meyer file."

"What?"

Prairie, sixty-five years old and verbally abusive, strode inside. I couldn't survive a single day without her, although I knew she wished I could, and *would*.

"Where did I put it?"

She shrugged. "Who knows?" She shouldered past me and shuffled papers around on my desk in search of the missing file.

A man carrying an enormous number of roses poked his head in my door.

"Emily Cartwright?"

"Down the hall, the last office on your right." My head buzzed and my heart raced. I followed him quickly, while managing to stay a safe distance behind. Several coworkers eyed the explosion of red and smiled, making comments as he passed by.

"More roses for Emily."

"God, who is this guy?"

"I don't know, but she should tell Jack to go fuck himself once and for all."

Laughter. I smiled, unable to hide my eagerness. The man stopped at Emily's door and I made myself comfortable among the other waiting women.

"Emily Cartwright?"

"Yes?"

"Delivery."

She walked to the door and the group of female coworkers moved in unison like a gossip crazed little herd, coming to a stop just outside her door. Emily's face flushed and every emotion was plainly visible. She was taken aback, overwhelmed, and obviously very moved. Her eyes searched the three dozen roses and a hand came up to cover her mouth as she took several steps back.

"Is there a card?" She seemed to know the answer, but a hint of anxiety was still apparent in her voice.

"Yes, ma'am."

I knew what it said and repeated it to myself as she opened the envelope to read it.

Emily,
A modest representation.
Of your every breath.

She slipped the card back inside the sleeve and her hand trembled as she laid it next to the flowers. She stood staring at them, wordless, as the man tipped his ball cap at us voyeurs and exited the office.

"Well, did he sign his name this time?" Val wanted to know.

"No." Emily turned, her eyes distant, searching for answers she knew she wouldn't find here.

"How do you know it's not Jack playing some sick game?" Val's secretary, Diane asked.

Emily shot her a look. "Jack can barely spell his own name. He could never express himself with words, with words like…" She stopped, drew a deep breath. "And he would never spend money on flowers."

"No," Val affirmed, "this guy's different." She walked to Emily's desk and lightly touched the flowers, a gleam of appreciation in her eyes. "He's bright, sensitive, and passionate. And madly in love with you."

"Mmm." Emily stood staring through the large office window. I watched her intently, knowing she was in a world that I had created. For the briefest of moments, we were there together.

"Expensive wine, poems, letters, roses," Val went on. "I would say it's all terribly clichéd if it wasn't so damn *good*."

"Yes, I know." Her attention lingered beyond the window, beyond the streets, beyond the cars. "It, all of it…it's like this person knows me. Really knows me." She paused, as if trying to make sense of it all. "And cares."

Silence filled the room, thick as fog, while the women all nodded and sighed.

"Does Jack know?" Diane asked.

"Yes." It was a whisper but heard by all. "His private investigator filled him in."

"He's giving you hell over it?"

Emily looked to Val and the gray of her eyes looked like mist mixed with rain. She was lost and alone. My heart shuddered at the sight.

"He's convinced I've been cheating too."

I nearly fell over with devastation. My doings had caused

her trouble. *Oh God.* She was suffering even more at the hands of her husband because of me. I felt sick.

"Okay, okay, break it up." Prairie startled us all, brushing past me, shooing the other women away. "There's work to be done, ladies." She paused next to Emily and spoke in a gentler tone. "Here's the Meyer file." Emily turned and took the file slowly, offering Prairie a tired smile. My secretary glanced at the desk covered in red and snickered. "I thought it smelled like a funeral home in here. This secret admirer of yours needs to show some guts and 'fess up or get lost. God knows your life is troubled enough."

Upon hearing that last statement, I turned and made my way back to my office. Everything I had tried to do, tried to share, had blown up in Emily's face. This game I had been playing, been gambling on, was now over. I had taken the risk and failed. I could no longer pretend that I lived in that world where Emily and I could coexist in love and in happiness.

❖

The steady pelting rain did little to soothe my pain. It slammed against my floor to ceiling windows and sloshed down in thick ripples to fall and rage in fast moving puddles on the street. Lightning flashed, brightly and briefly illuminating my loft, as if rudely reminding me of my empty bed with a merciless flash photo. I leaned upon the cool glass, helpless before the pain, hopeless that it would ever end. I couldn't sleep and hadn't been able to for days.

I missed her. Even though we worked in offices a mere fifty feet apart, I'd made it a point to avoid her. And it was killing me, my invisible cord to her torn.

I stared into the wine as it did its best to comfort me. Edith Piaf sang to me in sultry French tones, seemingly aware of how bad I was hurting. I took a long, warm sip and closed my eyes. The splattering of rain, the scratchy croon of old vinyl being read by a needle, the dark, rich taste of Silver Oak—they should have been enough to soothe me to sleep. But even though my body *did* grow weary and heavy, my heart still bled.

I walked to the night table next to my bed where I refilled my glass in the candlelight. Thunder growled in the distance and trailed off into a faint knocking noise. I cocked my head, curious as the noise became more of a presence. I glanced at my clock. It was midnight. A weeknight. The sound grew louder.

Who the hell could it be?

There, through the tunnel of the peephole, stood a figure framed by the dull glow of the hallway light. A lone, shadowy figure. The Silver Oak and I decided we didn't care who it was. Together we were fearless. I unlocked the door and turned the knob.

The door opened slowly. An inch at a time. And then, it stopped.

I blinked. I disbelieved. I blinked again and stared.

Emily.

Dripping wet.

Long coat and short midnight hair, slicked back against her head.

Full, deep red lips.

Piercing, hurricane eyes.

The wine glass, full and crimson, fell from my hand.

It broke on the wood floor. Loud but far away.

I blinked again.

Emily. Emily. It was Emily. Was it really her?

"Hello."

Yes, it was her. The sultry, throaty voice. I couldn't speak. She seemed to understand this and stepped inside.

"Do you mind if I come in?"

She was dripping and cold with rain. I could feel the chill and smell its earthiness as she moved past me. No umbrella. Just her and the coat and the rain.

"Yes, of course," I somehow said. I eased the door closed and turned to face her, too stunned to think about anything other than the way she looked.

She held my eyes as she took a step toward me, her words searching.

"Do you like my hair?"

The question seemed so out of place, that for the briefest of moments I feared I was imaging the entire thing. She lifted her hands to her hair, where her fingers ran through it.

"I got it cut. I needed a change." She trailed her fingertips slowly over her damp neck to the coat, darkened with moisture. "I've been wanting to do it for a long time. I've been wanting to do a lot of things for a long time." She paused. "Do you like it?"

My eyes were fixed on her lips where the question birthed with smooth, seductive tones. I swallowed hard as lightning flashed in her eyes. She'd brought the storm inside with her.

"Yes." The whisper floated from me, raw and exposing.

She seemed satisfied with my answer and undid a button on her coat as water continued to drip onto the floor with a steady patter. She should have been shivering, trembling with cold, but her body resonated with nothing of the sort. She was slick with wet, yet electric with humming energy. I felt it. As if she were a live wire, dangerous and whipping against the shiny black pavement, ready to strike if I stepped too close. She took another step closer and I caught sight of her shoes. High heels. Red. They seemed ill suited for a cold, midnight visit in the penetrating rain.

"What are you doing here?" The pieces of the puzzle were falling around me, slow drifting snowflakes settling to rest on the floor, but I couldn't yet put them together.

She studied me with deliberation. Her cool eyes seemed to breathe heat upon my skin.

"You stopped."

I stared, confused.

"You stopped," she repeated. She worked the remaining buttons open, but held the ends of the garment closed. "It's been two weeks. No wine, no roses. No letters."

Blood pounded to my head, hot and thick. Panic, adrenaline, fear, excitement. All of it felt fast and heavy as it slammed through me. *She knows. Oh God, she knows.*

She slid her hand down the outside of the coat, withdrew a folded piece of paper from the pocket, and held it out to me. Her voice was soft.

"I've come for my last letter. The one Prairie found in your office. The one you never sent."

I started to speak in defense, but she stopped me with powerful words of her own.

"I've been living for your words, Brynn. And lately, dying without them." She held my eyes with a determination I had never seen.

"Read it," she commanded with a whisper. "I need to hear you read it to me."

I focused on the familiar piece of paper, still folded neatly despite being crinkled with wear. I opened it and gasped as the words written in my hand jumped out at me.

"Read it," she said again, nearly breathless.

Her eyes bored into mine and her lips parted slightly, beckoning me.

I lowered my gaze and cleared my throat.

I spoke, my voice trembling:

Emily,
Red.
Lace.
Rich like velvet.
Dark and smooth and satin.
Teasingly covering her creamy skin in seductive webs of deep ruby.

My lips sucking through the satin lingerie.
Her neck, arching and showing itself, paling from the moonlight as her head tilts back in pleasure.
Her hair, cascading over her shoulders like ocean waves inked by night.
Red.
Clinging to her skin.
Dark and moist from my mouth.
Red.

As I finished the final lines, I heard her reciting them with me. She repeated the last of the words over and over while her hands opened the raincoat. The poem seemed alive and hungry, stealing the breath from my chest, squeezing the blood from my heart.

The coat fell to the floor.

I fought for air as the image in my mind, the one my words created, focused into this new reality, this new world with new boundaries.

"Is this..." she whispered. "Is this how you imagined me?" She stood as still as the night, her creamy skin moist and glowing in contrast to the dark red lingerie. Fingers splayed, she ran her palms up and down her body, over the lacy bra, across the planes of her abdomen, down to the lacy red panties.

"Tell me, Brynn. Tell me what you've wanted to tell me for so long."

My breath hitched in my throat. My heart thudded like mad against the restricting fingers of the poem. She was there. She was beautiful. Jesus-fucking-Christ, she was so beautiful. She was everything.

"I..." No words would come. After all the thoughts, the feelings, the letters, no words could ever come close to expressing what I was feeling at that moment. It was as if everything in me was strained and stretching. My muscles, my bones, my insides.

She had her hands inside me, pulling and clenching, killing me softly. My blood and skin felt white hot, burning in waves and waves of flushing heat. Somehow she was doing all this to me just by standing there, damp and red, breathing the same air as me and staring into my eyes. The red heels moved her closer and she took my hand and drew me toward her, seeming to understand. She leaned in, a mere inch from me, and I could feel the flames of her breath on my ear.

"If you can't tell me…then show me."

Her perfume hit me hard and fast. My legs trembled and I rested my hands on her shoulders for support. She took in another breath as the heat of our skin collided. She was damp, warm, and waiting. I groaned as she pressed into me, wrapping her arms around my neck. She felt so good against me. So incredibly soft and slick and warm. Soft was her skin, slick from the rain, warm from her heart.

"I've never been with a woman, Brynn. But I've thought about it…I've thought about you…for a long time." She paused, her breath tickling my ear. "When Prairie saw how miserable we've both been and she gave me the letter…something strange happened inside me. Just knowing it was you, all that time. It… did something to me." She brushed her cheek against mine and brought her lips a mere centimeter away from my mouth. "Kiss me."

Her breath teased my lips, and I couldn't get it into my lungs quickly enough. Gently, I skimmed my hands up her neck to her face. I needed to hold her, hold on to the moment forever. Lost in the allure of her scent, I lowered my head and felt her quiver as I touched my lips to hers.

Rich. Thick. Warm. Wet. Her moan fanned my flame. She pressed into me harder and the kiss grew deeper. My flame was now a raging inferno. My mouth came to life on its own and took her, one luscious lip at a time. First the top, then the bottom. Then her tongue. It came searching, and then came finding. I met it with my own and we became one, tasting and testing. She was sweet and slick with a darting, daring hunger. The feel of her so passionate, so ready, it was…unbelievable. I groaned and held her tighter, desperately validating her presence.

As if she sensed my need to feel her, she grabbed my wrists to lead my hands down to her hips. Then she whispered her fire in my ear. "Make me red. Red, just like your poem. Color me with your mouth."

As the request registered, my entire body ignited and pulsed. A rush of sound, like a crashing ocean wave, flooded my ears and I could no longer hear, and no longer cared. The image of her words was all that I needed.

I gripped her firmly, running my hands over her backside and squeezing. She threw her arms and legs around me as I lifted her off the floor. Teeth nipped at my neck as we spun, her tongue playing with my ear as I walked. I made it to the window where I pressed her against it and she gasped from the feel of the cool pane.

Rain still splashed against it. I kissed her again, hard and furious, as I rocked into the damp flesh between her legs.

Her fingers scraped my scalp and knotted in my hair as the kiss grew wilder and hungrier. I conquered her mouth and battled her tongue, swirling and swirling. I couldn't get enough, couldn't get deep enough. We fed on one another, so hard and relentless my lips first burned and bruised then numbed and tingled.

When she yanked me away by my hair her lips were dark and dangerous, lipstick smeared.

"I can't stop shaking," she said, and seemed strangely frightened, but her voice was deep and strong.

"Hurry," she demanded, pushing me away. I took a step back and lowered her to stand on her own. She gripped my forearms and seared her eyes into mine. "Make me red."

My world burned. I took her hands, laced them in mine, and pressed them over her head. I held her there, so long and so tight,

I swore I felt my fingers melt through the glass, felt the biting rain stinging my knuckles. Fighting with reality, I lowered my head to her chest. I felt her heart pumping wildly. I imagined I saw it as I pulled away, neon red and rushing, held captive against the cold, dark windowpane. I kissed her hot skin up to her neck where I sucked and licked where her veins fed her life. She cried out with pleasure as I fastened to her.

"Yes, yes," she panted. "You feel so good."

I pulled away and looked at her flesh. It was red.

Hastily, I pulled aside her bra and exposed her tan nipple. Her breath caught in her throat as my mouth colored her nipple to resemble her neck. She arched into me and ran her fingernails over my back. I sucked her hard and bit her soft. Her groans grew stronger and I released her hands. She clawed and commanded, first insisting then begging.

I worked my way lower, licking her clenching abdomen, kissing my way down. Her panties were satin and lace, hinting and teasing with the dampness of her desire. I kissed her there, where everything gathered and bunched, the nucleus of her.

She cried out, throaty and loud. "Oh God. Mmm. Feels so good."

The red material darkened with the moisture from my tongue. It was what I had dreamed about. What I had wanted for so long. She was here. It was happening. She was a beautiful dark red rosebud, and I was going to make her bloom.

I pulled down her panties as she tugged at my hair. She wanted more, wanted my mouth on her bare flesh. Her eyes were smoky and hazed, her head resting against the window. She looked at me when she stepped out of the lingerie. Her bottom lip trembled. It was an image I knew I would never forget.

I placed my hands on her thighs and breathed against the dark pink flesh between them. She shivered and moaned as her hand tightened in my hair. She wanted it. Wanted me. I could feel it humming out of her, but I needed to hear her say it.

"Do you want my mouth on you?" I whispered.

She licked her lips and leaned her back against the window once again, the feel of my breath driving her wild.

"Yes," she managed and then groaned, pulling me to her.

I resisted, my own body ready to burst from the inside out. I could almost taste her glistening, waiting flesh. "Tell me, Emily. Tell me."

She tilted my head to look at her. "I want...I want your mouth on me." Her eyes pierced into mine, so alive with need it took my breath away.

"Please, Brynn. Now."

Again, she tugged me to her, and this time I let her. Closing my eyes, I felt her hot flesh touch my nose, my lips, and my chin. I didn't move, but rather let her move me where she wanted me. She held me firmly while moaning and thrusting into my face, desperate for me to fasten to her. I inhaled her scent and moaned, relishing in the feel of her all wet and silky, all over my face.

When I felt her nails in my scalp and heard the crack in her voice, I knew neither of us could wait any longer.

I extended my tongue and licked her up and down, starting from the outside and moving in, barely rimming her hard clitoris. She shuddered and her knees nearly gave out, her body sinking against me. I held her up with all my strength, one hand on her hip, the other pressing open her thigh. Her moans grew louder as my tongue framed the length of her, thriving on her sound. Her clit was firm yet delicate, protruding and pulsing.

"Oh, Brynn."

I looked up. Her eyes were clenched shut, her chest expelling ragged breaths. "So good. Feels so good."

Dying to give her more, I moved my tongue lower and found the essence of her waiting for me, warm and ready and already pooled. It was milky sugar. The sweetest sugar I had ever tasted. With my head spinning, I flattened my tongue and spread her sweetness all over her excited flesh. She trembled as I feasted, first in a slow, gentle manner and then in a pressured frenzy, sucking in her flesh, again avoiding the clitoris. Her body jerked and pushed and then pulled and fought. She was going mad with desire, crying out into the night, beckoning to the resounding thunder.

Unable to hold off any longer, I took her stiff clit between my teeth and held it there as she gasped and slammed her head back. She bit her lower lip and her pelvis trembled against me.

"What are you doing to me?" she rasped.

I swirled my tongue over the tip and she bucked three times very quickly, unable to control herself. My mouth licked and sucked, swirled and stroked. I pulled away and saw that her flesh was a deep red.

I entered her, as many fingers as she could take, wanting to feel her bloom from the inside. She was hot, liquid silk, and I groaned at the feel of her spongy, firm tunnel. I thrust into her long and slow until her cries became short and fast.

The rose was unfurling.

Slowly.

Beautifully.

Rich and red.

I closed my eyes. I could see it there. Blossoming. I wanted to taste it. Taste the velvet red of the rose. My lips found her and fed. Yes. Yes. Beautiful rose.

"God, oh God, oh God!" Her cries ripped from her chest and the thunder echoed her as she came in my mouth, clenched around my fingers. She shoved herself against me, desperate and demanding. The pleasure I had given her had built and built and now it was bursting free. She was giving that to me. Her pleasure. And I took it, as much as I could. Swallowing it down. Swallowing her.

When my name sang from her lips in a soft, stuttered song, I slowed my tongue and eased my lips. The thunder that had echoed her trailed off into the distance and her fingers relaxed to stroke my hair. I pulled my mouth from her but left my fingers deep inside. She opened her eyes and brought her hands to my face, clasping me gently.

I waited for sweet nothings, for the declarations of love or emotion that often followed an orgasm. Especially one induced for the first time by another woman. But again, Emily Cartwright surprised me.

"Brynn."

"Yes."

"You made me red." She stared at me with eyes still heavy lidded with desire, but liquid like the glass splattered with rain.

"Yes, I did." Gently, I eased out of her and watched as a lingering spark of pleasure lit her face.

A serious look came over her and she ran her fingers across my lips as if they were her eyes and seeing me for the first time. A tear gathered and fell down her cheek. Concerned, I thumbed the warm trail away from her face.

"Are you okay?"

She stared deep into my eyes.

"Nothing's ever felt so good." She reached for my wrist and squeezed it tight. "I want to feel you inside me. Always."

I swallowed at her request. "Anything. Anything for you."

She smiled.

"Then take me to the bed and do it again. Make me red."

B IS FOR BEAUTIFUL

"Whatcha doin' today?" My great uncle Marty wanted to know as we loaded my small, seen way better days Geo Metro. That was his trademark question, calling every single family member who wasn't long distance every day asking, "Hey, whatcha doin'?"

I crawled in behind the wheel and started the car as he pushed in the lighter button and lit a cigarette. He smoked as I drove through the tiny Southern town in which I and everyone that had any drop of blood in relation to mine was born. I relaxed and breathed in the country air as Marty held his cigarette by his face, pinky extended. He held his beer that way too, way up high chin, pinky out.

"I don't know," I finally answered. I had been in town for a week and I was already feeling overwhelmed. "I think I might go for a drive." I just needed to be alone for a while. The funeral had been long, sad, and drawn out. Where I'm from wakes last for hours, the line extending out the door. Everyone comes dressed in their Sunday best, taking your hand in both of theirs, giving their condolences, and then they stand by the coffin and whisper, "Don't he look good? He does, he looks good."

"Can I come?" Marty asked, reaching out to rub the dash. "I like this car." He began turning the radio knob.

"I think I want to go alone." I switched on the radio for him. "But we'll do something tomorrow."

He nodded and smoked some more. "I'll call you tonight."

I knew he would, regardless, so I said, "Okay."

I relished Marty's unusualness. He was by far the most interesting person I knew, related or not. As weird as he was, he'd always been good to me and good to my mother. He was a devil on the guitar and he used to play little concerts for me when I was a kid. I'd sit on his squeaky bed in his small room, my feet dangling as the old air conditioner in the window ran. He'd tune his guitar and sing Elvis for me for as long as his voice held out.

We drove on down the road and passed the one swinging stoplight to turn into my grandmother's dirt road. As I pulled into the gravel drive I counted five other vehicles. Family and friends were still hanging out, stuffing the old Frigidaire with mountains of fried chicken and casseroles. This morning I even noticed a red velvet cake on the kitchen table.

"I'll see y'all later," I said as Marty hopped out and unloaded the tater tots, hair dye, and other personal items he'd claimed he desperately needed. He'd been spending the days at my grandmother's, along with everyone else. My grandfather had been a good friend to him and his sudden death was a shock to us all. I knew I should go inside and visit with everyone, but I was exhausted and finally grieving. The last thing I wanted to do was break down in front of my grandmother. She was having a hard enough time.

I watched as the strangest man I knew headed into my grandmother's house, accepting that he was probably saner than me. He, at the very least, had been married at one time. Me, I couldn't even claim a long-term relationship. But no one knew the true reason why. They all just thought I'd preferred college first before I settled down with the right man. I guess that's why I enjoyed time with Marty so much. We both held deep secrets.

I drove back up the dirt road away from the overcrowded farmhouse and then turned onto the main highway. The day was hot and muggy, typical for July in the South. I hadn't been home for a few years and I had no idea where I was going. Turning on the A/C, I decided on taking a scenic rural route. I merged off the highway and drove for over half an hour on a winding narrow road. I carved through trees, dense forests, and kudzu and then the road opened up onto vast green pastures before narrowing back into woods again.

Janet Jackson was singing about "Nasty Boys" when my car starting hesitating. Immediately, I switched off the radio and looked to the gauges. My engine temp was way up; something was wrong. I felt the air coming from the A/C vent with the back of my hand. It was blowing hot.

"Shit." Up ahead I saw an old gas station next to a weathered rusty building. "Come on, come on." I started jerking in my seat, as if that would somehow help. My eyes scanned the garage and I noticed a faded OPEN sign in the window. I craned the steering wheel into the drive just as the car died.

I tried the ignition but nothing happened. Smoke began to rise out of the hood. There was no movement from inside the garage, and I began to wonder about the sign as I took in the stacks of worn tires and grass overgrowing on the concrete. Without the A/C, the heat was stifling. I was just reaching to roll down the window when someone smashed against it, hands flat, nose smeared.

"Jesus!" I jumped.

"Overheated?" He smiled, kind of goofy looking but friendly. His hands were covered in grease and he had on a stained T-shirt. He backed away so I could roll down the window.

"I think so." I offered a smile of my own. He looked to the hood and then poked his head inside my window. I leaned back, slightly offended at his proximity. He clicked his teeth as he studied the gauges and then turned his head to look at me, his nose an inch from mine. Again the smile. He smelled like car grease and bubble gum, and I noticed a used sucker stick tucked behind his ear like a cigarette.

"I think so too." He backed out and opened the door for me. "Pop the hood first."

I did and then crawled out to watch him, wiping my brow. As he fanned away the smoke and leaned in, I heard the sound of water spraying. I turned slightly, to focus on the side of the garage. Standing in the shade, spraying herself with the hose, was a sight I will never, ever forget.

She was tall, about five foot ten, wearing cut-off jeans and a white sports bra, hair short and dirty blond in color. She was grinning into the white mist, her toned, somewhat muscular body glistening. Having thoroughly soaked her bra and shorts, the water was running down her legs to her Doc Martens boots. She didn't seem to mind.

The young man was saying something to me, but I wasn't paying attention. I was too busy watching her. She seemed to sense this and lowered the hose, turning off the water at the squeaky spigot. When she stood, she ran her hands through hair and smiled at the feel of the water sloshing down her back. My heart stood still at her smile and then I heated at the sight of her wet bra clinging to the small, taut breasts, their tips a dark rose.

She walked toward us and I smiled broadly as she approached.

"Overheated?" she said looking into the smoke pit of an engine, her nose crinkled.

"Yeah." He continued to fan away the smoke.

She sank her hands into her pockets and looked toward the sky, as if the sun were delicately massaging her face. "Don't open that radiator, Rudy. It's too hot. Let the engine cool down first."

"I know," he said, moving his hand that held the rag he was going to use to try to open it.

"I know you know," she said. "Just reminding you."

Rudy tucked the rag in his back pocket. "Sorry, ma'am, but

we need to wait awhile before I can get in there and fix it." He clicked his teeth again and dug in his pocket for a soft-looking cube of bubble gum.

"This is my sister, Iris." He happily chomped.

"Hi," I said, trying hard not to stare. "I'm Whit."

She turned her head but didn't look directly at me. "Hello."

We stood in silence for a moment and I thought maybe she'd seen me gawking at her and was offended. Again, I had to remind myself that I was home again and things were different here. I couldn't just gawk at every attractive woman I saw.

"You can wait with me behind the garage," she said. "It's cooler." She started to walk away and I followed, eyes trained on her bottom. We walked behind the garage on a well-worn path through the overgrown lawn to a tall, older home and a medium-sized shed beside it.

"In here," she said, opening the door to the shed and entering without turning around. I held open the rickety door and stepped inside. "Please close the door. Rudy will be out with your car touching it every few seconds until it cools."

I nodded and pulled it closed. The shed smelled musty with the faint scent of wet clay. Like the way an art room smells at an elementary school. It was considerably cooler, with a small air conditioner in the back window. The walls were white with beautiful colorful swirls painted throughout. Sunlight streamed in through the two uncurtained windows.

Iris stood at a large table, palms resting on its surface, her back to me. "Please come in."

I walked to the table and looked around at the shelves lining the left wall. They were covered in sculptures and busts, some of them fired and painted, some of them smooth and white.

"Did you do these?" I reached out and grazed one of a woman, beautifully detailed, breasts, nipples, musculature.

"Yes."

The table was covered in dried clay remnants but nothing else. She was staring at the back window.

"Do you think I'm beautiful?" she asked as if she'd just reached up and pulled the question from thin air.

I was completely startled, unsure I'd even heard her correctly. But the answer came out before I could stop it.

"Yes."

She was a golden goddess, bronzed and wet, shimmering in the flowing sunlight.

She cocked her head. "Come here."

I hesitated.

She pushed herself up and away from the table. "Please."

Swallowing, I stepped closer to her.

"Your breathing has changed," she said as her hand came up to touch my hair. I looked in her eyes, the ones that wouldn't look at me, and saw their unfocus.

"You're blind." It was a whisper, a surprise.

She laughed, throaty and deep. "And you aren't very perceptive."

My cheeks burned as my eyes devoured her hungrily, finally free to do so. Smooth and moist, her skin was sun-kissed and flawless, dark, honeyed freckles dancing across her nose. Her eyes were blue and endlessly deep, a shade I'd never seen before, like where I'd imagined Atlantis to be.

"You don't put chemicals in your hair." She paused and my eyes nearly rolled back in my head as she finger combed my hair. "You're trembling." She slid her hand down. "And you can't seem to breathe." She leaned in a bit and dropped her hand to mine. She turned it over and brushed her fingers lightly over my palm. My breath hitched. She smiled. "I know all about you now."

"You do?" I watched her lips—a soft pink—part slightly before she answered.

"Yes." The lips tugged at one side, amused. "You don't smoke but you were around someone who does. You're fairly young, mid twenties. Somewhat educated, you are from here but your accent gives away your home now. And..." Her hands drifted up my arms to my shoulders. Then, fleetingly, she touched my face. "You're very beautiful."

I closed my eyes, warming from her touch, nearly swooning as I leaned toward her.

"You like me," she acknowledged.

I opened my eyes, afraid. "I'm sorry I—"

Her fingers found my lips. "Shh." She lowered herself to breathe against my neck. A small noise escaped my throat at the feel of her breath. "Your perfume, I can't place it, but I like it." She straightened. "I want to sculpt you."

She gripped my shoulders and turned me so that my back was to the table. In a daze, I watched helplessly as she lifted my T-shirt over my head and tossed it to the side. My chest was heaving, the cool air kissing my back. Then her hands were at my shorts, unbuttoning and lowering. When they reached my ankles, her hands came back up to tug down the underwear. She was careful to avoid my skin, and I shivered, suddenly feeling self-conscious.

"Wait, I—"

But she shushed me again, finger on my lips. "Are you wearing a bra?"

I stared at her, my head buzzing. "No."

She inhaled through her nose and I saw her pulse jump in her neck. "Sit on the table."

As if I weighed nothing at all, she pressed her hands against my hips and lifted me onto the table. It felt rough and cold against my backside and I was about to protest when she cupped my face in her hands.

"What is Whit short for?"

I had to clear the rocks from my throat to answer. "Whitley."

Her thumbs parted my lips and dipped just inside, feeling my tongue. She groaned. "I'm going to touch you now."

She left me struggling for air on the table. At the shelves, her hands searched until she found what she wanted. Turning, she popped open the pink lid and squirted baby oil into her palm. My heart jumped.

"What's that for?" I could already smell it.

She held up her hand. "This is how I see. And this"—she held up the bottle—"this helps me to see."

She crossed the small room and stood before me. "Now, lie back and rest on your elbows."

I was already wet and I could feel it when I leaned back and stared into her face. The vein in her neck jerked every second and her lips were swollen with excitement. She rubbed her hands together and then held the bottle over me, squirting the cool oil between my breasts and down to my navel.

Her nose flared and her deep eyes flashed. Her breath hitched as she set the bottle down and then reached out for me. She started in the center, palms flat, and moved her hands outward. She smoothed her palms over me, up the planes of my stomach to my neck and shoulders, careful to avoid my breasts. She did this for a while, until we were both breathing heavy with desire. She raked her nails down the center of my chest.

"I can't wait any longer," she rasped. "I need to see you." Her tongue slipped out to lick her lips and she moved her hands upward. A loud groan escaped her as her hands slid over my breasts, slick with oil. She jerked with excitement.

"Oh God, I can see you now. Oh, I can see you." She moved her hands faster and in larger circles, exploring my upper body in a splendor I'd never seen. It was as if she were touching herself, her excitement growing and building. I arched into her, excited as well, feeling her hot hands slide over me and wanting so much more.

"You're making me wet," I said, wanting her to know just what she was doing to me.

She laughed and ran her hands up to my neck and held me a moment. "I know. I know."

Then, with another groan, her hands drifted lower and she

rubbed and squeezed my breasts and pinched my nipples. I cried out and reached for her head. I knotted my fingers in her hair as she went lower, rubbing my hips and trailing down to my thighs. She lowered herself and inhaled and then raked her hands back to my breasts.

"Oh, I can see you." A groan. "So beautiful."

I pulled myself to her, wanting to kiss her. But she planted her hands on the table and pulled away, my hand falling from her hair.

"Not yet," she whispered. She worked her way down my body again, her breathing rapid, her eyes wild. Her hands worked like magic, discovering and rubbing and giving and taking. She moaned as her palms rubbed my inner thighs and her thumbs lightly swept my hair.

I tried to sit, trembling. She continued to tease, lightly brushing over my pussy with her thumbs. Her head was tilted to the ceiling, as if she were giving thanks. She stood like that for what seemed like an eternity, gently teasing my hair, lightly teasing her fingertips.

"I'm throbbing," I said, unable to sit up, unable to take much more.

"Shh." She pressed into my shoulder. "Move back some more and lie down."

I was burning red hot inside, my pussy full and throbbing. My back to the cool surface of the table, I rubbed my hands over my slick breasts and watched as she gently spread my legs, placing my feet on the table.

"There," she said. "I want to see this part of you." She bent and breathed against my aching flesh. "I want to see every last bit." She spread me with her thumbs and we both cried out when she found my slick arousal. "Oh God, yes," she whispered. "This is better than oil." She turned her hand and dipped into my folds, rubbing up and down.

I pushed my hips in the air, hungry for it.

She bit her bottom lip as she worked me, holding it with her teeth. Then she lifted her hand and rubbed my juices over my breast, pinching and rolling the nipple.

"Whitley, you are so beautiful, so beautiful." She ran her nails down my abdomen and again spread me with her thumbs. She lowered herself to her knees and eased her nose into my hair. Another groan escaped her as she inhaled. "Oh God, you smell good." Her eyes closed, she pushed herself further in, rubbing her nose, mouth, and cheeks against me. An erotic laugh seeped from her throat as she rubbed her face into me like a cat rubbing on scent. "You are so wet, so wonderful."

My hands clawed at the dry surface of the table, flakes of dried clay coming undone. Her cheekbones were pressing into my clit each time she turned her head.

"Iris," I whispered, wanting terribly to grab her head and hold her to me so I could gyrate against her and come all over her face.

"Shh," she said again, sensing my excitement. "You are wet and thick, your flesh very full." She pulled back, holding me open. "I'm going to find you now." She stuck out a long tongue and flicked my tiny clit lightly. I jerked and moaned, thrusting into her. She laughed again and pressed closer, lapping at my clit. She flicked me again and again, so quick and light, her tongue like a machine. I could feel myself growing harder, growing larger, my small red tip extending outward, reaching for her tongue.

Oh sweet God, it felt so good.

"Mmm. So little and hard." She stopped her machine-gun assault and lapped harder and longer, using both the front and back of her tongue.

Oh motherfucker, her tongue was firm and wet and heavy, and I wanted more, would kill for more. Then she started to swirl. Great big wet circles all over my clit.

"Ahh!" I clawed at her head. "I'm gonna come," I warned.

She stood from her knees and wrapped her hands around my hips, lifting me with her. Her hungry mouth fastened to my flesh, she sucked me into her, holding me snug inside her mouth. Her tongue worked the underside of my clit while her lips and teeth dug into the top.

I cried out again and again, the feeling of being feasted upon overwhelming. Her eyes were closed and her hungry mouth made wonderful feeding noises as her head bobbed, sucking and pulling.

"Motherfucker," I seethed, coming so hard my head snapped back and my body strained against her. My nails clawed at the table and my eyes clenched along with my legs. I was tensing and dying, tearing at the table, coming in her mouth. The orgasm had built and built and then burst inside me, my flesh begging and stealing, needing more, more, more. Nothing had ever felt so good. Nothing.

She held me like that, to her mouth, until I finally stilled, heart racing, swallowing against a dry throat.

I jerked a few more times against her mouth, sensitive.

She opened her eyes and pulled her mouth away slowly. She licked her lips and lowered me back to the table. I could see the redness of her swollen mouth, the wet flush of arousal on her cheeks. She had me all over her face, glistening in the sunlight.

She smiled down at me and rubbed her hands over my breasts. When she twitched with delight I knew she was close. I sat up and scooted off the table. Her head followed me, but she said nothing.

"I want to touch you now," I said, reaching out with sore fingernails full of dried clay to unbutton her fly. Her hands ran through my hair as I forced down her wet shorts and found no panties.

I kissed her lightly on her thighs, working my way up. She groaned and pushed herself to me.

"Are you going to taste me?"

I could smell her arousal and see the slickness of it on her dark honey hair. "Yes."

She massaged my scalp and her breathing quickened. "I'm going to think about you every time I use the hose to pleasure myself."

The vision of her spraying herself with the hose came to mind. Then I imagined her holding the end of the hose inside her shorts, coming against the cool flow of water. I wrapped my arms inside her thighs then and held her buttocks to me. I pressed into her wet flesh with my tongue and found her clit large and full and waiting. Her nails dug into my scalp and she held me tight and I knew there would be no waiting. I took her in my mouth right away and sucked her just behind my teeth to the roof of my mouth. I played her with my tongue as I worked her like this, tugging her hard and fast. Her warm excitement spread over my chin, and I closed my eyes at the wonderful taste.

She began to groan, louder and louder, her hands running over my face, her fingertips at my mouth, feeling me sucking her.

"Ahh, ahh." She thrust into me, faster and faster. Her fingers pressed into my cheeks, trying to get to my mouth and I pulled away for a split second, letting her. Hurriedly, she moved her fingers to her clit, framing it with her fingertips. I licked at them hungrily and felt her twinge with need. Then I took her in my mouth again and sucked and swirled her clit with her fingers right there, watching.

She threw her head back and came loudly, stumbling backward against the shelves. I held her tightly and followed on my knees, pressing into her harder and faster. She continued to come, howling with a raspy throat, jutting herself into me. She pushed her fingers into my mouth and I sucked them off, swallowing the come right off them. Then I went back to her clit and did it the same. As she forced herself into me, her legs quaking, her come hot and slick in my mouth, I lowered my right hand from her backside and rubbed my own seeping wetness into oblivion once again. I came and pressed into her pussy, moaning and thrusting my face against her.

We both shook and groaned, holding fast to one another, our bodies tight and writhing like spent bows.

When my tremors stopped I turned my face and rested against her flesh, desperate for breath. She moved her hands and stroked my head, her own body still trembling.

"Whitley," she said, her voice deep and rough, so sexy because I knew it sounded like that because of me. "How long are you here for?"

I looked at her and licked my sore lips, her come thick and salty and sweet. "I'm not sure."

"Will you come back before you leave?"

I stood and leaned into her moist neck, unable to keep my balance. She shuddered.

"Yes."

Her hands found my face where they traced over my mouth. "Good. I want you to see your sculpture."

"You're still going to sculpt me?" She hadn't even started. We'd gotten too carried away.

"Oh, yes," she laughed. "I've got you all right here." She pointed to her eye. "I can see you forever now."

She brought me closer and we kissed, wet, glistening lips, tasting ourselves. She felt warm and inviting, her tongue a soft, firm velvet. I wanted to get lost in her forever.

As I closed my eyes and kissed her earlobe, I knew I too would hold her forever in my mind.

"I see you too, Iris. Always."

O IS FOR ORGASM

The attractive brunette walked out of the high-rise building at exactly twelve noon, just as she did every weekday at her lunch hour. With assured purpose she made her way to the sidewalk thick with vendors where she bought a diet soda and unwrapped a straw.

Across the street Lauren Canfield lowered her newspaper, crossed her legs casually, and took a long sip from her own straw. She watched as the brunette continued on past the food stands to a covered area where newspapers, magazines, and books were sold. Finding a column bookcase, she paused, rotating it slowly, plucking out a small paperback. Seeing her chance, Lauren lowered her newspaper and crossed the street.

"Looks pretty wild," she said, coming to a stand next to her. She sipped her drink nonchalantly.

The brunette's eyes quickly darted toward her but then just as quickly refocused on the book in her hands.

Lauren studied the bookcase, her free hand finding a paperback of her own.

"This one's good." She pretended to concentrate on the back cover. "Of course, that's only if you've already read Fuller. His Bradford series blows these away."

The brunette lowered the book in her hand and cocked her head. A smile eased its way across her face.

"You've read Fuller?"

Lauren nodded. "Sure. You?"

"I just finished the Bradford series."

Lauren met her eyes. They looked just as they had that first time she'd seen them a few weeks before, like sunlight through a jar of honey. She'd tried not to stare on that ride in an elevator, but now she looked for a good long moment and thought how everything about the brunette reminded her of honey, from her sun-streaked hair to her slightly bronzed skin.

"They're good, aren't they? The books," Lauren asked.

The brunette laughed with excitement. "Yes!" Then she seemed almost embarrassed at her reaction and she lowered her head. There was a long pause, and Lauren could almost hear her mind searching for something appropriate to say. It came soft and a little unsure. "So, do you read a lot, then?"

"Try to. You?"

"Every chance I get."

Lauren replaced the book and rubbed the back of her neck. "I'm usually so busy working...sometimes it's hard to find the time to read as much as I would like to."

The brunette smiled and it lit up her entire being. "I know how that feels."

"What do you do?" Lauren pretended not to know.

"Administrative assistant." She rolled her eyes. "Assistant my ass. I do *everything*."

Lauren laughed and shoved her hand into her jeans pocket, waiting for the next question, the important one. It came quickly.

"What about you?"

She looked out into the street, staring into oblivion. "I'm a photographer."

"Oh?"

Lauren couldn't tell if she was highly intrigued or disappointed. Usually it was one or the other. No in-betweens.

FLESH AND BONE

She looked to her once again and grinned. "It's a living. And it helps in my true passion. My collection."

"Like baseball cards or something?"

"Sort of." A long silence ensued when Lauren didn't elaborate. Not wanting to wait any longer, she went in for the kill.

"Listen, I would really like it if maybe you could drop by sometime." She reached for her wallet and rifled through it. "You've got a great face and I would love to photograph you." She plucked out her business card and held it out to her.

"You're kidding, right?" The smile was there but it was different.

"No, I'm not kidding."

The brunette looked around in frustration and then focused back on Lauren with eyes that were as rock hard as her face. "I thought only asshole guys used that line."

Lauren considered trying to explain but knew it would do little to calm her. Instead, she took her hand and placed her card in her palm.

"If you change your mind, give me a call." Lauren spoke softly, hoping it would resonate outward. "I can compensate you handsomely for your time."

She turned and walked away, stepping over the curb to cross the street. A cab sped by, allowing her the freedom to cross but she hesitated, hoping.

"Excuse me?" The voice came from behind. She turned.

"Yes?"

"You're Lauren Canfield?" Her face had softened considerably. "Lauren Canfield the photographer?"

Lauren relaxed. "Yes." She had heard of her. That always made things easier.

"I-I'm sorry, I didn't realize." She looked at the business card and then back to Lauren. "I'm flattered, I mean, you really think I'm good enough to photograph?"

"Absolutely."

She shook her head, not yet convinced. "All those models you shoot and everything…I don't know."

Lauren smiled, enjoying her modesty. She was, indeed, perfect.

Lauren spoke with reassurance. "I wouldn't ask unless I meant it. Give it some thought, okay?"

Another taxi passed by, and this time Lauren crossed the street leaving the brunette there with her card in her hand and no doubt numerous questions in her mind.

❖

Two days later, she called.

"Hi, I'm not sure if you remember me, I didn't even get a chance to introduce myself…"

"The Fuller fan." Lauren smiled and rose from the couch in her loft/studio. "Right?" She stretched, stiff from examining proof after proof on her light table.

"Yes. I wasn't sure you would remember me."

"Of course I remember you."

Silence. Lauren could sense that she was still unsure.

"Are you calling to take me up on my offer?"

There was more silence and then, "Yes."

"Excellent." Lauren spoke quickly, afraid she would change her mind. "When can you come over?"

"Well, I'm not sure. We're going to do this at your place?"

"Yes, I have a loft and I use it for a lot of my shoots." Lauren walked to her fridge and cracked open a beer, her mind already racing with the details of how exactly she wanted to photograph her. "I would like to do it around sunset if that's okay."

She stared out her vast windows, enjoying the rose and yellows the setting sun cast throughout the city.

"You won't be alone," she added. "There will be two others with you."

"I wasn't really worried about that." She paused. "Things are kind of tight right now. I just split up with my girlfriend and…"

"Money. Yes." Lauren swallowed some cool amber beer. "I can give you a check for three grand. That's for one evening. No strings. I keep one photo with your permission. You get the rest, hard copies included."

"That sounds more than generous." Her breathing changed. She was ready. "What should I wear?"

"Dress casual. Jeans."

"Jeans?"

Lauren laughed.

"When?"

"Tomorrow evening okay?"

"Yes."

"Seven?"

"Yes."

"Great, see you then. Oh, and what's your name?"

"Sorry?"

"Who do I make that check out to?"

"Therese. Therese Howell."

"See you tomorrow, Therese."

❖

She arrived early, knocking on Lauren's door at six fifty. She was obviously anxious, and that was always a good sign.

Lauren welcomed her inside with a smile and she stood just inside the door with a look of nervous apprehension.

"Wow." Her eyes took in the large loft, lit almost entirely by candles.

"Please make yourself at home." Lauren headed into the kitchen where she offered her a drink. "Merlot okay?"

Therese took a few steps in, still in wonder. "Sure."

Lauren handed her the glass and led her to where the two other women sat on the large cushioned couch.

"Therese, this is Bo." Bo stood and shook her hand, a sly grin playing along her face.

"And this is Carmen." Carmen gave a wave and a smile before crossing her ankle over her knee. Both were young, fit tomboys with sharp, androgynous features and short, thick hair that could be made to fit any look.

Therese smiled and fidgeted a bit, showing off her nerves. Lauren watched her closely, wondering what caused it more, the two tomboys who were just her type, or the fact that she would be photographed alongside them.

Wasting no time, Lauren moved to the built-in shelves on the far wall and switched on the stereo. After adjusting the volume she retrieved her camera and lightly touched Therese's arm.

"I thought we would start out here." She walked to the French doors and headed outside to the wide terrace that overlooked the city. The light was just right, like deep yellow roses with red tips. The buildings shimmered in the light, some silver, some orange. Therese stood by the door, seemingly taking in the view and breathing in the cool evening air. Bo and Carmen passed by her, one gently taking her hand to lead her the rest of the way out. She seemed a little surprised at the contact, but fell into step alongside them.

They stood toward the end of the terrace, the city and sunset bursting into the background beyond. Therese took a few deep sips of her wine, obviously still battling her nerves as Bo and Carmen stood next to her. Lauren approached, offering her a comforting smile as she took her near-empty glass and set it on a small table.

"There are only two things you need to worry about here, Therese," Lauren said. "One, relax." She approached again and began positioning her, moving her arms to help with the stiffness and fingering her hair to let some errant strands come down around her face.

"And number two?" she asked, breathing heavily as Lauren backed away.

"Have fun."

She nodded and took several quick breaths as Lauren paced and then squatted, searching for the perfect capture.

"Okay. Breathe easy, Therese," Lauren encouraged from behind her lens. "Let's go." At her command, Carmen tossed her arm over Therese's shoulders while Bo wrapped an arm around her waist. They leaned in with easy smiles, all in worn jeans, casual and sexy like they had been close friends for years. Therese wore a dark brown tank top that brought out the light brown sugarcane color of her skin and accentuated her eyes.

Lauren took shot after shot, hypnotized. Therese relaxed, following the lead of her seasoned companions. They laughed, held hands, embraced. Eventually, Bo took off her shirt, showing off her lean muscles and white sheer bra. Therese openly stared, seemingly mesmerized at the darkness of her nipples showing through the fabric. It was a pivotal moment and Lauren didn't want Therese to grow uncomfortable.

"Therese, why don't you come stand by me? I need some intimate shots here." Surprisingly, she seemed disappointed. She opened her mouth to protest but then thought better of it. With hesitance, she walked toward Lauren and turned to watch as Lauren continued to click away. Bo and Carmen immediately rubbed together, Carmen unbuttoning Bo's jeans with fingers that slid up and down her abdomen. They kissed, soft, slow, and teasing.

"Carmen, open your blouse a little."

She did as instructed and they kissed again, short, tugging kisses. Their hands caressed and searched, their bodies coming to life with the fire of desire. It was a beautiful scene with beautiful light. Lauren lowered her camera and found Therese watching intently. Brushstrokes of color darkened her cheeks, and she seemed to be holding her breath.

From what Lauren knew, it had been at least six weeks since Therese had experienced any intimacy. She had been holed up in her apartment all alone wondering where her relationship had gone wrong. And now, her desire, which had been buried deep with all the recent trouble in her life, was sparking to existence once again.

"Let's take a break." Lauren placed a hand on Therese's shoulder. She jerked, startled, and tore her eyes away from Bo and Carmen.

"I'm losing light," Lauren said, looking off into the growing night. "We'll have to go inside."

Therese nodded and the four went back inside the loft. Lauren busied herself readying her camera for more.

Therese seemed more at ease and even asked for more wine.

"Please help yourself. It's on the counter," Lauren said.

She continued working on her camera. After going over every photo, she ejected the memory card and inserted a new one. So far, the pictures had turned out beautifully.

Her equipment ready for more, she moved into the main room, turning on a few lamps as she circled the open space. The candles were still burning throughout the entire loft, flickering soft light. She pushed the plush red velvet couch from the center of the room to the back wall where the off-white drapes acted as a backdrop. She took a step back with her hands on her hips. Ready.

As she knelt behind a tripod, Bo and Carmen joined her, making themselves comfortable on the sofa. Therese came as well, standing next to Lauren.

"Your check's on the table," Lauren said, maneuvering the camera. Carmen and Bo seemed lost in their own world as they started touching one another with light, purposeful fingers, trailing up and down exposed necks and arms. Lauren didn't look away as her camera began to click.

"Pardon?" Therese asked.

"Your check. It's on the table. Along with the memory card with all the photos. I wrote down which one I would like to keep." Lauren glanced over at her. "With your permission, of course."

"You mean, that's it? I'm done?"

Lauren, changing her mind about the shot, released the camera from the tripod, and stood, moving closer to the models.

"Yep."

Therese was quiet, and Lauren could sense her hesitation. And maybe, just maybe, more than a little disappointment. Lauren looked at her and her face said it all.

"You did a great job."

She met Lauren's eyes but seemed to have no words.

"I hope you had fun." Lauren smiled, meaning it.

"I did," she said. "I had a lot of fun." The disappointment was high in her voice. "I just thought you would need me for more is all."

Lauren studied her for a moment, trying to see into her, to know exactly how she felt and what all she could and would be willing to handle.

"It's not that I no longer need you," Lauren said with soft sincerity. "It's that I didn't think you would be comfortable for these next set of photographs."

"Oh."

"But you're more than welcome to hang out for a while if you want."

"Hang out?"

"Sure." Lauren gave another smile. "And watch."

Lauren felt her answer, didn't need her to voice it. It was heavy and real, thickening the air around her.

Therese wanted to remain. She wanted to watch.

Lauren refocused on her models and nodded, camera ready. Carmen ran her hands up to Bo's breasts, massaging and pinching the nipples through the bra. Bo sighed heavily and the candlelight reflected the dance of their tongues.

Therese stood staring, mesmerized. Lauren moved about carefully, poised like a cat, capturing quickly and efficiently.

Carmen removed Bo's bra and tossed it aside. Her hands moved back to her nipples where they pinched the exposed skin for real. Bo cried out softly and reached for Carmen's shirt. She unbuttoned it slowly, tongue still dancing in her mouth as she did so. The flickering light caught Carmen's dark skin beautifully. Muscled shoulders and a defined chest came into view as the shirt was peeled off and tossed to the floor. The white of her bra contrasted sharply but shortly as Bo nearly tore it from her body. Carmen moaned a yes, helping to discard the bra, her mouth continuing to suck on Bo's tongue.

Lauren took shot after shot, moving quickly.

"Good," she said. "Good, now, Carmen, move behind her."

The two stopped kissing and Carmen stood and walked behind the couch. Bo faced forward and leaned back, welcoming Carmen's eager hands, which immediately began to massage and titillate. Bo's eyes fell shut as she moved with the caresses, arching her back and offering herself further. Carmen massaged and pinched her nipples, running her hands down her taut abdomen and back up. Then she dipped her head and kissed her neck and shoulder, at first lightly and then heavier, licking with her tongue and nibbling with her teeth. Bo reacted vehemently, grabbing a fistful of short kinky hair, pushing herself onto the back of the couch. She kissed Carmen back, still holding her head while her other hand hurriedly unfastened her own jeans once again.

Carmen roughly squeezed a nipple and Bo pulled away, crying out softly. They stared at one another, breathing rapidly, eyes burning. Carmen mouthed something, words of encouragement, of desire, of pleading, Lauren did not know. Then she took Bo's breast into her mouth, tugging long and wet on the center, causing Bo to release her hold and tilt her chin toward the ceiling. Then her hand drifted down to Bo's waistline where she slipped it inside her jeans and began to move it back and forth.

Bo cried out again and spread her legs. Carmen held her tightly, wrapping her other arm around her while she sucked on her breast and rubbed at her flesh.

Lauren glanced at Therese. She was standing very still, mouth slightly open, face flushed. Her eyes were intense and one hand was opening and closing at her side.

Bo tugged Carmen away from her breast and kissed her, tongues glistening in the light. Bo groaned and rocked a little into her hand and then they both looked to Therese, mouths moving with moans and impassioned pleas, eyes heavy with desire.

Carmen eased her hand from Bo's jeans and she moved it slowly, tracing up her torso to between her breasts and up to her neck. When she reached her mouth she spread her fingers and pressed them against her lips. Then she leaned forward and snuck her tongue out, licking her fingers and probing into Bo's mouth. The sight was stirring, torrid beyond words, reaching down into Lauren and clutching her stomach.

Next to her, a soft noise came from Therese, and Lauren watched as she raised a trembling hand to her mouth. The pulse that beat in the nook of her collarbone surged madly beneath her skin. Her tongue swept across her lips quickly. Then she took two small steps toward the couch without looking down, as if her body were on autopilot.

The models stopped, nearly breathless, and looked at her.

Bo stepped down from the couch and lowered her jeans. Her gaze was locked with Therese's as she eased out of them, one long leg at a time. She wore no panties and she stood unabashedly for a long moment until Carmen joined her, stepping out of her own jeans and panties.

They kissed again, more possessively, with teeth pulling on lips and tongues demanding entry. The air grew thicker, charged with the sounds of human lechery, wet, hungry mouths and moans and sighs and hurried breathing.

Carmen pushed Bo back to the couch where she again sat on the back of it, legs open. Carmen went around and again kissed on her torso, breast, and upper arm. She slid her hand down to her center, where she slipped it into her bare flesh to rub. Bo tensed and then relaxed against it, her bones suddenly melting. Soft moans escaped her and then she grinned and groaned and held Therese's eyes.

"It feels good," she said. "So damn good."

Lauren held her camera tightly.

"Can you see how good it feels?" Bo asked.

Therese stood staring, so still and erect Lauren knew she would tip at the slightest of touches.

Carmen stilled her hand and stepped onto the small stool positioned behind the couch. She ran her fingertips up and down Bo's sides and used her mouth on her neck and shoulders once again. This time she sucked harder, sank her teeth in further, and squeezed her nipples firmer. Bo called out, her face tight and her eyes closed. The sensations seemed to snap against her like a curling whip, straightening her spine and heating her skin.

She opened her eyes and looked to Therese. The grin was gone and in its place was a seriousness and a wanting so strong Lauren could feel it crawling throughout her own body, rushing to the pooling wet heat between her legs.

Bo's gaze continued to bore into Therese as Carmen fed ravenously on her neck and shoulders. Then slowly, Bo ran her hands up the insides of her own thighs. When she reached her flesh she slid one hand inward and framed her clit with her long fingers. She began to vibrate herself, jerking her fingers side to side in a rapid motion.

Quickly, she sucked in a sharp breath. Then she moaned and nearly shut her eyes.

"Come here," she said to Therese.

Lauren held her breath. Therese didn't move for a few long seconds. But then, slowly, she stepped forward.

Lauren watched, poised with pent-up desire. Bo urged her onward and reached out for her once she was at the couch. She pulled her forward and kissed her with eager lips. A long sigh came from Therese and she released it into Bo, who held her fast, tasting her and testing her for a long while before they parted. When they did, Bo lifted Therese's tank top from her body. Therese stood still and let her, and then allowed her bra to be removed as well.

Then Bo yanked her forward by the wrist and watched as Carmen too kissed her hungrily. Bo took advantage and sucked her exposed neck, causing her to sigh some more. She lightly caressed her breasts and pinched the nipples ever so slightly between her fingers.

Lauren clicked away, focusing on the moving muscles of Therese's back as she took in the pleasure. Therese was breathless when Carmen pulled away and even more so when Bo looked at her and said, "Now your jeans."

Therese didn't seem unsure but rather unable to make her body follow commands. Her hands no longer trembled, but they were slow moving and clumsy as she fumbled with the buttons.

Bo slid off the back of the couch and sat in front of her. She held her hands and looked at her.

"Do you want me to do it?"

Therese breathed deeply. "Yes."

Bo released the buttons and slid the jeans down carefully. Lauren moved to the side and readied her camera as Bo lowered the panties.

When she was completely nude, Bo appraised her with first her eyes and then her fingers. She traced her skin up and down, whispered words only Therese could hear, and then lightly kissed her abdomen.

Therese inhaled and held her head, allowing her eyes to fall closed. Carmen moved from behind the couch to behind Therese where she placed her hands on her hips and trailed light kisses of her own down her back. Therese stiffened readily as Carmen ran her tongue first down and then up the center of her back.

Bo quickly stood and went to the side of the couch. Swiftly she pulled a lever and lowered the back so that it lay flush with the front. The red velvet was now more like a bed, vast and shimmering, waiting and wanting. Bo lay on it, head toward the front, and Carmen took Therese's hand and led her on with her knees.

"I want you on me," Bo said, holding out her hand. Carmen crawled further on and settled between Bo's legs, licking hungrily right away.

"Please," Bo said, the pleasure quickly overtaking her. "I want you to feel what I feel."

Therese watched as Carmen spread her further open and flicked her tongue back and forth hurriedly. Bo tensed and faded, crying out softly.

"I've never done this before," Therese said softly, eyes still trained on Carmen's tongue.

Lauren lowered her camera, more than surprised and confused as to exactly what she meant.

"Never?" Bo asked.

"No."

"Why not?" Bo tightened her hands in Carmen's hair, trying to still her, but Carmen wouldn't let up.

"I've never allowed anyone before."

Lauren knew Therese didn't stay in relationships for very long. Now she had a hunch as to why.

"But this," Therese continued, looking at them all very slowly. "This is different."

Lauren's mind searched for meaning, trying to understand. There was no one judging here, no one asking for her heart, for her life, for her devotion. Here there was only pleasure and beauty, completely wild and free, captured only for a moment and then set free again.

Carmen finally stopped and rose to her knees. Therese met her gaze and leaned toward her, closing her eyes. As the distance between them grew shorter, so seemingly did Therese's resolve. And when they met, they kissed, and Carmen nearly fell forward as Therese took hold of her lips in a fury of built and released passion.

She was tasting Bo and Carmen together and she did so with a new hunger. One that came with groans of lust and hard, fast thrusts of her tongue. Bo sat up and joined in, kissing Therese's breasts, eagerly pulling them into her mouth and then swirling her tongue around each nipple until Therese grabbed her head and held her away.

"Something's happening," she said, her voice unsteady. "I'm feeling everything here." She lowered her hand to her center, where her light brown hair was curly and moist. Bo lay back down and reached for her hip.

"That means it's time," she said. "Come here."

Therese hesitated for only a split second and then she straddled her and allowed Carmen, who straddled Bo's torso, to help her move forward. Her thighs trembled as she rested her knees near the sides of Bo's face.

"Now," Bo said, encouraging her. "Lower yourself to me."

Therese eased downward and Bo groaned in a welcome, pushing out her tongue to lick her right away. Therese cried out a little and then closed her eyes as Bo licked harder and then took her clit into her mouth and sucked.

"Oh, oh my — oh my God." She pressed her lips together and tightened her eyes. Tendons in her neck stood out as she began to pump her hips over Bo's face. Behind her, Carmen massaged her breasts and bit and sucked on her neck. She whispered words of passion and hunger into her ear.

"Something's—something's happening," she said as Bo sucked on, wrapping her hands over her thighs. Lauren heard Bo release briefly and she caught sight of her tongue as Therese rubbed her flesh against it, forward and back and back and forward. Then Bo refastened and Therese quickened her hips.

"Oh God, oh yes, like that. Please, like that."

Carmen held her tighter, her arm curved up and over her

shoulder. Therese bucked like she was on a horse, one hand loose, her arm flailing. Her torso flexed and her breasts swayed. She licked her lips and then bit down on them.

"What's happening, something's happening. Oh, it's getting bigger. Bigger. Oh." She jerked her hips and her eyes flew open. She locked them with Lauren. "It's coming, oh God, it's coming. It's—" And then her mouth fell open and her eyes widened even more and she rocked and rocked, neck strained with small, hard sounds coming out of her chest. Then her eyes squeezed shut again and in another split second they flew open and she said, "Oh, Lauren," and another wave of pleasure ripped through her again. She jerked even faster, whipping her hips, fucking Bo's face.

"I—I—oh God. Oh God!" And then another came and she slowed her hips and moved them slow and hard and very purposely all over her face. "Yes, oh God, yes," she said, fucking Bo's mouth long and slow. "Oh fuck, take me, take all of me." And then her body went slack and Carmen wrapped her in her arms and held her tightly.

The room went completely silent. Therese slouched, chest rising and falling quickly. Bo moaned and snuck her tongue out for a few more random licks, causing Therese to jerk and beg for her to stop.

After several moments Carmen eased her backward and they both sat next to Bo, who sat up and smiled. In a surprising gesture, Therese reached for her face and kissed her and then she watched as Carmen kissed her too. The three leaned on one another and laughed softly. Carmen said something amorous and kissed Bo again, pushing her back down and positioning herself between her legs, eager to finish the job. Therese watched in glazed amazement, looking very much like the lazy smoke of a spent firecracker.

But when Bo came she was right there, at her mouth and she kissed her, seemingly wanting to take it in and swallow it down deep. Then she watched again as Bo sat up and fucked Carmen, shoving her fingers up and in and out, so hard and fast Carmen was crying out in Spanish. When she came, Therese was there with her as well, kissing her, holding her tight, swallowing the pleasure down whole.

They kissed and kissed and Therese couldn't seem to get enough. She was breathless and limp when they pulled apart, yet she was flushed and her eyes were ablaze and seeking.

Legs weak and unable to stand any longer, Lauren set down her camera and pulled up a chair. She crossed her legs against her pulsing flesh and lit a cigarette and inhaled deeply. She watched with desire as Carmen and Bo lay Therese down once again. This time they spread her open as far as she would go and they both went at her clit with their tongues. Flicking and teasing and pressing and licking, tongues fencing for the clit, attacking the sides and teasing the tip.

Therese thrashed her head and strained her neck, grabbing both their heads and clenching their hair. They brought her close to orgasm quickly, and then Bo pushed inside with her fingers and Therese nearly sat up and called out in ecstasy, her throat sounding tight and hoarse.

The cry stretched and broke, and she bucked her hips wildly and clung to them for a long, long while before the cry fell from the air altogether, swallowed by silence and the flickering of the candlelight.

Lauren sat and watched, taking in the beauty of the desire and the passion. She extinguished her cigarette and stood, retrieving her camera.

❖

She had been in her makeshift office for almost an hour when Therese came looking for her.

"Can I come in?" She was dressed, but her face was still flushed and her neck was smudged with vampire-like kisses.

"Sure." Lauren rubbed the back of her neck and stood, new

memory card in hand. She gave it to Therese. "This has all the latest." Therese took it slowly and began to look around at the two walls. Frame after frame hung side by side, wrapping around the room. She went to each one and stared, some of them she touched lightly with her fingertips.

"Your collection," she said, finally looking back at Lauren.

"Yes." Lauren joined her. "And if you don't mind, I'd like to add yours to it."

Therese laughed softly and then stopped when she realized Lauren was serious.

Lauren turned her laptop around. "This is the one I want."

It was Therese, on her knees, back arched, torso flexed, eyes open with pure uninhibited pleasure. Her mouth was slightly parted, the tendons in her neck taut, just before she was about to call out.

The photo was Therese at her deepest, darkest level. She was coming and coming hard.

"That was my very first time," she confessed, almost as if to herself. She traced a finger over the image of her face. "I'd never come before."

Lauren knew it was special. It was the best photo she'd taken thus far. Beautifully raw and captivating. A real woman coming for the very first time.

"It's something, isn't it? The way we all look when it happens," Therese said, glancing around at some of the other photos.

Lauren agreed. "To me it is the most raw, uninhibited, stunning, and stimulating moment I could ever capture."

Therese met her gaze and then looked back down at her own image. "Yes, it is, isn't it?" She paused, as if lost in thought. "You want this one?"

Lauren swallowed hard, the photo playing the chords of her libido just as the live version had. "If you don't mind."

"You won't use it anywhere else?"

"It will hang on my wall and my wall alone. Forever."

Therese nodded. "Okay."

Lauren smiled. "Thank you, Therese."

Therese returned it with a tired, easy smile of her own. "No, thank you." And then as her smile grew into a grin, her eyes sparkled, and she asked Lauren for one last request.

"You watched me, now I want to watch you."

N IS FOR NAUGHTY

For the last two days, only two words ran through my mind.

Franco Saulis.

He was worse than most, a man who benefited by controlling others. Namely, human slavery in the form of prostitution. The women he took were young, many of them underage. He kept them by physical force, brainwashing, and good old-fashioned threats to their lives.

Unfortunately for most, one or two of those threats were continuously carried out regardless of performance.

So when I arrived at his house, I felt a wonderful buzzing of anticipation and the metal like taste of vengeance on the tip of my tongue.

Outside his house just after midnight, all was quiet. The skeletal palo verdes and mesquites blew in the oven-hot breeze. He lived out in the desert where the earth was parched and desolate, where anything in existence that ever wanted to thrive would never want to be. Strangely, I felt right at home.

I moved like the night, quiet and dark, first killing his power and then entering his garage, where I shoved open the folding door. I worked swiftly and hurriedly, setting up my grand stage and readying it for the show. Then I entered his house by cutting a small circle in the glass of his back door through which I slipped my hand in and popped the lock.

The security alarm beeped when I opened the door, but I was expecting this, knowing his brand of alarm well. Through the kitchen and living room I went, hurrying down the hallway.

I found him at the alarm panel in his bedroom, nude and cursing. I switched on my strong flashlight, and two young, frightened prostitutes screamed and jumped from the bed when they saw me.

"Turn off the alarm," I said, pulling my Glock from my dark jeans and aiming it squarely at him.

He jerked and held up his hands, his face cowering from the light. His body was what I call skinny fat, long and thin, but saggy, covered in ugly, coarse black hairs. He disgusted me on many levels, and I had to look at his face and clench my jaw in order to not turn away.

"Turn it off," I said again. "And you better only push four buttons." When he remained still with his hands up and trembling, I fired a shot and hit the top of his foot. He screamed like he was being skinned alive and I rushed at him, forcing the gun to his temple. "Do it," I said.

Whining loudly, he typed in the code and dropped to cradle his bleeding foot.

I swung around to the girls. "Get dressed."

They obeyed quickly and I pulled Franco up by his ear.

"To the garage," I instructed, walking behind them, gun aimed at the back of Franco's head. He limped and sobbed, begging and pleading at me. His spine was as weak as his soul.

We walked inside the open garage door and I showed off all the explosives I had planted. I openly admired his classic cars, focusing on his new Shelby GT, which I knew was not yet insured.

He was already crying when I shoved him over to his standing safe. With my gun pressed to his head, he opened the door with unsteady hands. I counted a hundred thousand dollars or so and had the girls drop the stacks into a black trash bag. I gave the last stack to them and told them to share it and to take off. They were now free.

One cried and the other thanked me profusely. Neither said good-bye to Franco as they hurried from the garage.

"Well, I guess it's just you and me, kid," I said, staring at his skinny legs covered in a swarm of black hairs. I forced him outside and we faced the garage. Standing there in the dry desert dirt, I fished in my pockets and pulled out a cluster of handheld explosives.

Kneeling, I began to tape them onto his penis, grateful to be wearing my leather gloves. Sobs shook his body, and when he realized what I was doing, he pushed me away and tried to run. I picked up my gun and shot him again, this time in the ass and the back of the leg.

He took a few more difficult steps, collapsed, and cried some more. I shoved him onto his back and finished taping the explosives on. Then I made him sit up and I forced a detonator in his hand.

Immediately, he shook his head and drooled out some no, no, nos.

"Push the fucking button," I said.

He cried harder.

"I don't have all night, Franco. Push the fucking button." I shoved my Glock to his skull.

"I'm sorry," he cried. "Tell Tiny I'm sorry. I will leave the girls alone."

"It's too late. You've done your damage. Now pay the price."

"No, no, no. Please. I swear to you. I will stop."

"No more girls," I said.

"I swear."

"Ever."

"Okay."

"Your days of pimping and abusing are over. Say it."

"Yes, yes, I swear. Please." He fumbled with his penis, trying to strip the explosives off. But his fingers didn't want to work.

"Are you telling the truth?"

"Yes." His body quivered and slimy drool stained his chest, reflecting the moonlight.

And then he peed.

Sighing, I took the remote from him and told him I believed him. He seemed relieved and surprised so I continued, remembering three dead girls and dozens of others, raped, beaten, and abused.

"But just in case you're forgetful, here's what's going to happen if you go back on your word."

He screamed as I pushed the button. The garage rocked with a massive explosion. The ground shook, knocking us both back. A huge fireball rolled up into the dark sky.

Getting my bearings, I stood and found Franco curled in the dirt sobbing, his hands cupped over his penis. The heat from the flames pressed against my skin as I nudged him with my foot.

"Get up, motherfucker." He rolled over, his face contorted with fear. He moved his hands and sobbed some more as he found his penis intact.

I bent over him and stared hard into his eyes.

"Keep your promise, Franco. Or next time it will be your dick."

My name is Diem Rushton. I am a vigilante.

❖

The next day I entered the gentlemen's club through the large double doors and squinted into the vast dim room. The cool air attacked the thin sheen of sweat on my skin, threatening to freeze it rather than evaporate it. Casually, I wiped my brow and made my way to the bar, the black trash bag in hand.

I panned the room, more than a little disappointed when

I didn't see the sexy brunette who sometimes waited tables. Instead, I noted the black shiny catwalk glimmering under the colorful lights, and I counted eight bald heads bobbing at stage level. Loud music started over the speakers, the bass thumping quickly as I eased myself onto a high-backed stool.

The bartender recognized me and slid a cold Miller Lite into my hand. I took a swig and turned back toward the stage. A curvaceous little blonde pranced down the runway and grabbed on to a pole. Her large breasts, too perfectly round to be natural, continued to shake as she swung herself around.

"Diem!" Next to me, a strong hand gripped my shoulder. I lowered my beer, and club owner and longtime friend Tiny De Martino cupped my face with his short, stubby fingers. His hand was warm and soft just like his eyes and he smelled strongly of Drakkar Noir.

"My girl," he said to me with great affection. "Come, let's make words."

Per his usual, he led me across the room on quick-moving legs. We went through a doorway and down a long hallway lit with weak lights positioned above the baseboards. Turning right we entered another dim room with large leather chairs, a couch, and a few small lamps on accent tables. It smelled different from the main room. Less stifling cologne and beer and more like the subtle fresh rainforest air fresheners you hang on your rearview mirror. I liked the room much better than the bar, having been in it at least a dozen times before. Tiny always feared that his actual office was a target for listening devices, so he held meetings with me in here where they swept daily for bugs and admittance was strictly regulated.

"Sit," he said, pointing to the large couch. I eased onto the leather cushion and watched as Tiny did the same, the stereo remote in his hand. After turning the powerful system on and adjusting the volume to voice level, he turned sideways and wiggled his eyebrows.

"Franco is so mad." He slapped his short thigh and laughed heartily. His pant legs rose and I smiled back, amused by his orange and black striped socks.

"You shouldn't have any further problems with him," I said. I handed him the trash bag full of cash. "Here's some severance pay."

Tiny dug through it, his eyes lighting up like a kid on Christmas morning. He handed me three stacks and set the bag aside.

"I thank you, Diem. I thank you so much." He hugged me, little arms wrapped around me.

Franco had caused him a lot of trouble. Seducing his girls and then holding them hostage, forcing them into his prostitution ring. Tiny was good to his girls and he thought of them all as his family. Losing them to Franco hurt his soul, and he feared for their safety. He had paid for and stood at attention at more than one funeral.

"I owe you. I owe you too much." He laughed and stood, bag in hand. Walking to the door, he turned and said, "But today I have a surprise. Wait here."

Five minutes hadn't even gone by when she entered, all things sex wrapped into one.

"Hello," she said, after closing and locking the door. She stared at me and stood still, allowing me to take in her short dark hair, big brown eyes, thick lips, and lengthy five-foot-nine body.

"Hello." We'd never spoken before, just held brief heated gazes as she busily waited tables.

"I heard what you did," she said, walking toward me in a short dark skirt and gray sleeveless blouse.

"Just doing my job."

She stood before me and looked into my eyes.

"It was a job very well done."

She smiled and I caught her scent. Calvin Klein's Eternity.

She reached for the remote and switched the tuner over to a

CD. As the silence searched for the sound to start, she returned the remote and reached down to stroke my face.

"I'm here to thank you."

I swallowed hard. "You don't need to."

"I know. But I've been wanting to talk to you. So when I heard what you did, I told Tiny I wanted to personally thank you. With a private dance."

I struggled for my voice. She didn't normally dance. Only waited tables. Tiny had said she was a grad student with a healthy amount of self-respect. He made sure others *respected* that.

The music started. She turned it up nice and loud and Beyoncé's "Naughty Girl" began to pound out.

Her hand left my face like a whisper and she started moving her hips. My skin began to burn, and she shoved me back against the couch and started in on her blouse. One button at a time, painfully slow, she gyrated and opened her shirt. Her face was serious in a sexy seductiveness, lips pursed slightly, eyes blazing.

Down and down her hands went, peeling open her blouse and skimming her defined abdomen. Palms flat, she moved them up and down and then stripped the shirt from her body.

I inhaled sharply, hit at once by the beautiful glow of her amber skin against the black satin bra. Then down went her palms again, this time to her skirt, where her fingers undid the clasp and her hips shook it off, one inch at a time, eventually revealing a pair of matching black satin panties.

My heart thudded into my throat and all the way out to my fingertips. Her eyes held mine captive as she slid the skirt down and off her legs. Then she swung her hips to the beat and straddled me, grabbing my hands and placing them on her ass. Her body tightened as she moved, waving herself into me, her spine as limber as a snake.

I flushed and burned hotter, the scent of her as real and as powerful as the heat of her skin. She put her hand on my shoulder and arched into me again and again, like she was riding in a saddle and moving with the beast beneath her. Her ass was round, soft, and full. My clit ached as I held her buttocks like two fleshy globes, feeling her every move and sashay.

I imagined smacking it in the heat of lovemaking, of sinking my teeth into each cheek as she came.

As if hearing my thoughts, she groaned and bent down to my ear.

"Squeeze me harder," she said as she reached back to unhook her bra. With it loose she lowered her arms and pulled it slowly from her chest. Her eyes scorched me as she slipped it off and tossed it aside.

A short, sharp breath escaped me. Her breasts were the size of my hands, the nipples dark like fudge. My mouth at once watered and she again grabbed my hands. She placed them on her, each one cupping a soft, weighty breast.

She sighed and thrust her chest forward, stretching her neck back. She held my wrists and moved them faster, encouraging me to massage her. Then she looked at me and pinched her nipples from between my fingers.

"Ah, ah, yes." Her body kept moving, dancing into my hands. Her eyes fell closed and she pinched herself again and groaned. She held my gaze as she moved. Told me without words what she liked and what she loved. What she longed for and had to have.

I squeezed my fingers, holding her nipples captive. She cried softly and pressed her hands over mine, rubbing herself. "Baby," she said, breathless. "You're about to get one hell of a dance." Then, with another groan of desire, she stilled our hands and crawled from me to stand.

Music still throbbing, she again moved her hips and rubbed her palms up and down her body. She moved so fluently and so seductively, it was hard to believe she didn't do it for money. She was made to move, built to seduce.

She continued to stare into my eyes as she danced, hands drifting to her panties. There she dipped her fingers into the waistband and pushed them down. Down, down, down they went. Off one long, graceful leg and then the other. I studied the glimmer of her waxed skin, the sleek muscles of her thighs.

She watched me as well, spinning her panties around her finger before tossing them into my lap. Then, with another smoldering look, she turned around and danced, running her fingers through her hair and down the sides of her body. They played over her hips and then rounded the curve of her ass. She shook it to the beat, short and sexy and then longer and hypnotizing.

I breathed heavily through my parted lips, awakened and consumed by her. She turned her head, glancing at me from the side. Throwing me another grin, she bent over, touched her toes, and then flexed upward, parallel to the ground, dipping the small of her back.

She waved her body again and came back up slowly, gripping her ankles and then skimming her hands up her legs as she went. She turned and slapped her ass, watching me closely from the corner of her eyes.

I sat gripping my thighs, the satin panties softly kissing my skin and my heart running away with my libido.

Another firm slap made me blink and she turned, deliberately and slowly. Facing me once again, she danced and slithered, the music somehow moving through her. Her hands went low to her pussy and teased with her fingertips. I saw the glint of slickness below the short hairs and I knew she was just as excited, that it wasn't all an act.

A hot shot of thrill surged through me and I felt my eyes narrow in further desire. Her catlike body continued to move and she could see the change in me, I could tell by the way she parted her lips and lifted her hand to her mouth. Her pink tongue came out and licked her front two fingers.

Then slowly she lowered them, trailing them over her skin to her pubis once again. There, she first sighed and then she touched herself.

I let out a noise myself as I watched the two fingers strum alongside her clit, mingling with her wetness, opening up her soul. Her flickering brown eyes spoke of the pleasure's welcome, allowing her fingers to stroke the inner chords of her desire.

She took a step closer, her need mounting. She stilled her hand and brought it to my face and pressed it to my lips.

"Taste," she mouthed and I did so at once, running my tongue along her fingers, tasting her sweet arousal. Her eyes flashed dangerously and she straddled me and grabbed my hand.

Hurriedly, she pulled it toward her center, shoving it into her painfully wet and hot flesh. She took my cheek in her other hand and made small noises as she stared into my eyes.

"Inside me," she breathed. "Now."

I strummed her flesh up and down and then dipped the tips of my fingers to her opening. She held me tightly, one hand squeezing my shoulder, the other gripping my wrist.

"Please," she begged.

With two fingers I went inside, and she sank down on me with a groan and an internal clenching.

"Ah, fuck," she whispered, shoving her hips back and forth. She wrapped her other arm around me and leaned in as she desperately rode my fingers. "You make me feel so naughty," she said.

And then she straightened her arms and leaned back, bouncing up and down on my fingers, using her thighs as springs. I curled my fingers and pushed against her walls, flicking the tip of her cervix back and forth.

Her nails dug into my upper arms and her abdominal muscles tightened like she was doing sit-ups. She called out over the last of the music.

"Yes. Ah, fuck, yes. Yes!" And then she screamed and

bounced and yanked herself up to me where she singed me with a deep, hot kiss.

Her body continued to move as her tongue swirled and her lips captured. Madly she thrust, until her body gave in and went limp atop me. She tore her mouth from mine and audibly gasped for breath.

Soon the room was quiet with only the deep rhythm of our hearts beating. I could feel hers pulsing around my fingers. She raised her head and looked into my eyes. Hers were watery but starkly clear, as if they'd just been washed and she was able to see through them for the first time.

"That was so bad," she said, laughing. And then, with a deepening of her strained voice she added, "And so very good."

She leaned in and bit my neck, causing me to jerk.

"Do you know what I'm thinking?" she asked.

I watched her closely, in awe of her even then at her most vulnerable. She looked at me with openness, with honesty, with her same consistent confidence.

"No."

"I'm thinking I want more." She trailed a finger down my cheek. "I'm thinking I want those thumbs." She eyed my hands. "I'm thinking I want them on my clit."

"Yeah?"

"Yeah."

"Do you still want me inside you?"

"Yes."

Carefully, I placed my thumbs along the sides of her clit. She pulsed her hips and sighed.

"Yes, oh yes. Right there."

I rubbed her, massaging her hot full cleft, pressing into it along the sides, feeling it twitch. She laughed as she moved.

"It's good. Fuck yeah, it's good. Mmm, can you tell how well I like it? Am I tight around your fingers? Am I soaking them with my excitement?"

"Yes."

"Do you like it? Do you like the way I feel?"

"Yes."

"I love the way it feels." She kissed me, sucked hard on my bottom lip. "I want to taste you. I bet you would taste so good right now." Her hips quickened and I knew she was close. I could feel her cinching around my fingers, feel the swollen heat of her flesh between my thumbs. "I want so many things. But I'm going to wait. I'm going to wait until I can get you all alone in your bed."

She reached for my face, held me captive with her hands and eyes. Her hips jerked and she struggled for breath.

"And then I'm going to spread you open and taste you—" She neared climax as she spoke. "Going to—oh God—lick you and suck you—take you in my mouth—make you come with my tongue—"

She stared fiercely into my eyes as her body convulsed all around my hands.

"Would you like that?"

My voice had vanished.

"Tell me," she demanded.

I nodded and swallowed with difficulty. "Yes."

She threw her head back and cried out. "Oh yes, I'm thinking of you…of you."

Her hands slipped from my face to cling to my shirt as she leaned back, the last of the orgasm claiming her.

Her chest heaved and her skin glistened. Her stomach was taut, a faint vein running down into her hip.

Silence filled the room. The music had stopped. My hand ached but I hadn't noticed until now. All I could feel was her. Wrapped down on to me. Hot and tight. Insanely wet.

When her eyes opened, she slowly pulled herself forward. Her fingers remained tightly clutching the fabric of my shirt. She smiled coyly.

"What are you thinking right now?" she asked.

I was thinking many things, but one in particular. "I'm wondering why you work here." She belonged on a real stage, on a movie screen, in front of a classroom, or at the top of a high-rise building…in my bed, in my life. She didn't belong here.

"I need the money," she said simply. "Men tip more when there's a naked woman on the stage."

"You don't dance," I stated.

"No. And I won't."

I smiled. "You did for me."

She laughed and kissed me softly. Her voice was ragged from spent passion, and nothing had ever sounded so sexy. "You're not a man. And I told you before, you make me feel naughty."

She released my shirt and pressed her palms over it in an attempt to smooth it out. She did the same to my lips with her fingertips.

Her eyes told me she had more to say, but instead she climbed off me and stood to dress. I watched, knowing that I could for all eternity and it still not be enough.

"So, do many people make you feel that way?"

She refastened her skirt. "No." Her mouth tipped mischievously. "Just you so far." She bent and retrieved her bra and wrapped it around her waist to fasten it. As she turned it around and slid her arms into the straps she said. "How about you? Do you normally go around beating up bad guys?"

"Yes."

"Oh, so this isn't just a one-time gig, then?" She picked up her blouse and slipped her arms through the holes.

"No." I stood, not wanting her to go. The feeling was new to me. Exciting and terrifying.

"Well, then," she said as she buttoned. "Looks like we both have our naughty little secrets. I work here, and," she pulled me into her arms, "you make the world a little safer."

She held my hand and pressed her lips to my palm. I answered by kissing her lips and cupping her ass.

She moaned and laughed softy as we pulled apart.

"Can I see you again?" I asked, at that moment wanting nothing more.

"You don't even have to ask. I meant what I said."

"That wasn't just the heat of passion?"

She grinned and slid her hand down the front of my jeans. I gasped when she found my flesh.

"Oh no. That was a promise." She removed her hand and licked her lips. Then she kissed me one last time and headed for the door.

"Only next time," she said, "you owe me a private dance."

E is for Everlasting

Chandler Brogan awoke in the dark to the phone ringing. Groaning, she stuck her hand out from beneath the covers and searched for the receiver.

"Hello?" She barely sounded human.

"Hi."

Chandler opened her eyes and pushed herself into a sitting position.

"Hi."

"Come to the door."

Chandler switched on the lamp and rubbed her sleepy face as she stood. She knew that voice, would know it anywhere.

"Okay." Her heart rate kicked up considerably as she blinked her eyes and crossed the room. The floor felt cool against her feet and she kept the phone snug to her ear, her way of ensuring that the connection was real and not a dream.

Reaching the front door, she flipped on the porch light and looked through the peephole, a habit she found herself doing despite knowing who exactly was at the door. It wasn't just because Michael, the ex-husband of her friend and colleague, had tried to kill her. It was because she was awakening nights to the sound of the doorbell, and she wasn't sure if it was a dream or reality. Whatever it was, dream or not, the front porch was always bare by the time she reached the door.

Pushing her concern to the back of her mind, she noted the familiar figure beyond the door and turned the lock. Her insides leaped beyond wakefulness as she pulled it open.

There, in the weak halo of light, stood Sarah Monroe in worn jeans, boots, and a faded denim shirt. The deep dark of night outlined her form, seemingly tempting her to take a step back so it could swallow her whole. Fucking gorgeous didn't even come close to describing her at that moment.

"Hi," Chandler whispered.

Sarah smiled. "Hi."

It had been three long days since Chandler had seen her, and the vision of her standing there at her front door with wet black hair as dark as the night and cool blue eyes as pale as her shirt was beyond anything dreamlike. She nearly pinched herself.

"You're here," she said, lost for words.

"Yes." Sarah took a step forward and leaned on the doorjamb. She smelled of Pert shampoo, and Chandler knew she'd just finished her shift at the Department of Public Safety and had most likely showered there in the locker room. Lately, she smelled of Pert and Irish Spring when she finished a shift. Chandler couldn't yet smell the soap, but her nerve endings were jumping for the opportunity.

"Tomorrow evening seemed way too f―――," ――― said, her eyes sweeping Chandler up and down, taking in her tight gray tank and blue plaid flannel pajama bottoms. "I've missed you."

Chandler reached out for her hand and gently pulled her inside. "I've missed you too." They'd both been busy with work and Sarah had been working nights, helping out her understaffed department.

The overtime showed itself in the shadows under her eyes. Chandler wanted to smudge the darkness away with her thumb as she watched her close and lock the door.

"Are you hungry?" They walked further into the house and Chandler stopped at the kitchen. Her cat Mitote flicked his tail lazily from his position on the back of the couch. He extended his chin eagerly as Sarah reached out to give him a scratch.

"No."

"Thirsty?"

Sarah looked her up and down again, this time amorously. "No."

Chandler felt her skin tingle, as if Sarah had already stroked her.

"You sure?"

Sarah held her eyes and stepped closer to her quickly, pushing her against the wall in the entrance to the hallway. She pressed her palm into her chest and stared at her lips for a long moment before looking again into her eyes.

"I think you know what it is I want, what I need. And it is far more demanding and insistent than the need for food or water."

Sarah's intense passion was something she was just starting to get used to. And she was loving every minute of it.

"It is?" Chandler whispered, lost in the flaming yellow circles that surrounded the pupils in Sarah's eyes. Sarah always left her speechless. And breathless.

"Yes," Sarah said on a quick breath just before she took her lips with her own.

Chandler moaned slightly and tangled her hand in her hair. The chill of her damp hair contrasted sharply with her impossibly soft and achingly warm lips. Her seeking tongue tasted of cinnamon, just like the gum she sometimes chewed while doing paperwork at the department.

Chandler relished knowing these small personal habits and she pulled her closer, unable to ever get enough. From the first moment she'd seen her nearly a year ago, walking up to her in her khaki uniform and citing her for excessive speed, to pushing her against the wall and awakening her innermost desires, none of it was ever enough.

"Mmm, oh God," Sarah said, pulling away. "I can't believe how much I've missed you."

"Me neither." Chandler stroked her strong jaw. She saw the want and need staining her cheeks. She felt the strength of her tight, muscular body, saw it deep in her eyes, eclipsed by something more hidden but ever present. Vulnerability.

"Come here." Chandler led them to the bedroom and turned to undress Sarah slowly, starting with the long-sleeved denim work shirt.

"I love the way your eyes shine when you wear this," Chandler said, moving her fingers down button by button.

"I love the way you look at me when you tell me you love me," Sarah said.

Chandler smiled. "I love you."

Sarah touched her cheek. "I know. I love you too." She pulled the shirt from her arms and watched as Chandler undid her jeans and led her to the bed. When she sat, Chandler pulled off her boots and socks and then helped her out of her jeans. She was on her way to extinguish the lamp when Sarah stopped her and stood.

"Wait."

Chandler looked at her, standing still next to the bed.

"What is it?" Sarah looked so serious all of a sudden, standing there in her white bra and white boy-style briefs. She walked over to Chandler and took her hand.

"I want the light on," she said.

Chandler thought it might be another request to help deal with all the abuse she'd suffered at the evil hands of a family friend. But when Sarah looked into her eyes and Chandler saw the flash of desire's flame, she knew it had nothing to do with him.

"I'm ready," Sarah whispered. "For it."

Chandler understood at once and her heart somersaulted in her chest. "Are you sure?"

"I've never been more sure. I've been thinking about it all day. It's about to drive me insane."

"Okay."

Sarah had come a long way and now she was ready to climb over that last obstacle, the one that promised the ultimate intimacy, if she could just hurdle over the past and get some leverage.

"But I want the light on. And I want you close to me, as close as you can get."

They had discussed this many times before. And Chandler knew exactly what it was she needed and how. Sarah wanted her close, but she didn't want her looking at her face. She needed to feel this on her own and decide for herself how it felt and what it meant.

"Okay." Chandler kissed her softly. "Whatever you need." She placed small kisses on her neck and firm shoulders. "You just tell me."

Sarah smiled and her eyes were close to tears. "I want to see you." She peeled Chandler's tank top over her head and then ran her fingertips over her breasts and down to her abdomen where her fresh red scar slashed over her skin. "I still hate the thought of this," Sarah said.

"We all have our scars," Chandler said. "Some just show better than others. This one." She touched her stomach. "It's only skin deep."

"I wish mine were," Sarah said.

"They will get better. Give them time," Chandler said, meaning it.

Sarah slid her hands slowly downward and tugged Chandler's pajama bottoms and panties down her legs and off her feet. Then, standing very still, she allowed Chandler to help her out of her bra and her boy briefs and they both stood there nude, staring into one another's eyes.

"I'm ready," Sarah said, reaching out to cup her breast, rubbing her thumb over the nipple. "I'm so ready."

Chandler sighed and she felt her eyes widen in desire. Hurriedly, she shoved the pillows against the headboard and pulled back on the sheets. "Sit down with your back to the pillows," she instructed, rifling through her nightstand drawer. Finding the black leather harness, she dug further and retrieved two phalluses, one black, one white. Holding the black one, she anchored it to the harness and then swung it around backward and secured the buckles.

Sarah watched her closely as the phallus hung from Chandler's backside.

"Trust me," Chandler said with a small grin. Then she handed over a tube of lube and turned around until she felt the mattress against the backs of her thighs. "Go ahead," she said.

She heard Sarah move and she felt the phallus being tugged on as she covered it in lube. She couldn't see it, but the thought and feel of it alone sent pings directly between her legs.

"Are you finished?" Suddenly she could barely seem to control herself. She wanted to turn the harness around and mount Sarah quickly, shoving the cock deep inside…

"Yes," Sarah said.

Chandler put the tube on the nightstand and stilled her trembling hand. "Do you like it? The cock? I bought it with you in mind." It was a smaller-sized phallus than the white one.

"Yes," Sarah said again.

Chandler looked at her over her shoulder. She swallowed. "Okay, now sit back and spread your legs."

Sarah hesitated only a second and then did so. Chandler crawled on and sat in front of her, with her back to Sarah, scooting back to between her legs. When she got close she instructed Sarah to grab hold of the cock.

"Now, as I move back, guide it into yourself, okay?"

"Okay."

"Take your time. Don't force it."

Chandler heard her breathing, clipped and ragged. "Oh. Kay."

Chandler backed up some more and placed her hands on

Sarah's thighs. She felt her hard muscles contract and watched as her heels dug into the bed.

"Take your time, baby. We have all the time in the world."

She stroked her thighs, running her fingers down to her knees and back up again.

"Mo—re," Sarah said and Chandler pushed back a bit more. She could feel her hot breath on her shoulder, feel her cool breasts touching her back. Then she heard another quick inhale and exhale and Sarah grabbed her, hugging her arms around Chandler's chest and yanking her back.

"Sa—rah," Chandler rasped, surprised. But Sarah let out a long groan, low and deep and then Chandler felt her hot mouth bite into her neck.

"Sa—rah," she said again, caught up quickly in her passion as she hugged Chandler tight and cinched her legs around her.

"Ah, ah, Chandler," Sarah said, her calves flexing and her toes curling. She bit Chandler again and then hurriedly rubbed her hands over her breasts to capture her nipples.

"Are you okay?" The question was dumb, Chandler knew, but she was struggling to catch up and she wanted to make sure.

"Yes, ah God, yes." Sarah moved against her, trying to fuck the cock. "What, what now?" Sarah asked. She had told Chandler exactly what she wanted, and Chandler had planned out this position on her own, specifically for this occasion. Sarah was climbing the obstacle quickly, seeking the next step.

"Does it hurt?" Despite Sarah's excitement, Chandler wanted to be careful.

"A little. But it—it feels good more than it hurts."

"Okay," Chandler said. She leaned back against her, loving how her breasts and abdomen had heated and now felt warm against her skin. Chandler opened her legs, placing them over Sarah's. Then she grabbed the white phallus and said, "I'm going to put this in me now."

"Yes," Sarah encouraged. "Please do."

Chandler pushed it up and in and she closed her eyes briefly at the feel of it. Then she began fucking herself softly. "Touch me now," she said, guiding Sarah's hand. "Touch me while we fuck."

Sarah groaned as her fingers found Chandler's wet, slick flesh. She encased her clit and stroked her up and down and then all around.

"God, yes," Chandler said, the pleasure mounting quickly. Sarah's fingers played her expertly, long and nimble, holding her clit prisoner, moving it whichever way she demanded.

"You're fucking me," Sarah whispered in her. "Oh God, you're fucking me." They moved into a rhythm, Chandler pushing backward and Sarah thrusting her hips forward.

"Yes, I am. I'm fucking you, baby. And I'm fucking myself too. Look." Chandler pointed at the standing mirror positioned in the corner of the room.

"Uh," Sarah moaned. "I see us. I see you." She quickened her hand on Chandler's clit and pinched her nipple harder. Chandler cried out and arched back into her.

"Oh, Sarah. Jesus Christ, yes."

In a frenzy, Sarah stopped, lifting her hand to lick her fingers. She groaned and told Chandler how good she tasted and then put the fingers to her mouth so she could taste for herself. With both cocks still fucking, Chandler stuck out her tongue and then took Sarah's two fingers into her mouth and sucked.

"Fuck, Chan. Ah fuck."

Chandler bobbed her head back and forth, sucking her hard. Sarah bucked into her harder, legs squeezing in on Chandler while Chandler's own heels dug deep into the mattress. Sarah's leg muscles strained along with her voice and Chandler released her fingers, knowing she was close.

They found her flesh at once and resumed their magical travels, framing her reddened clit and then rubbing all around it in quick circular motions. The sensation sent Chandler catapulting toward climax and she shoved her cock in further and faster, completely caught up in the large fire she and Sarah were creating.

"Yes, Sarah. Please, baby, yes, come with me."

Sarah's groans turned to grunts and her eyes bored into the mirror, staring into Chandler's soul.

"Chan—Chan." Her muscles tightened, her toes curled so tight they whitened from lack of blood flow. Her hand moved from Chandler's breast to cinch her tighter across the chest.

"Chan I—it—Chan."

"It's okay, Sarah. Let it go. Let it feel good."

"It does—it feels—I feel full."

"I'm feeling the same thing. The very same thing."

"Oh God. Chan—Chan—you feel it?"

Chan quickened her own fucking. "Yes, I do. Can you see me?"

"Ye—yes."

"Do you see my cock? See it fucking me?"

"Yes. Ah yes."

"I'm pretending it's you. Wishing it was you inside me."

"Ah, Chan—oh God."

"That's it, baby. I'm coming too. Come with me."

"Chan—"

Chandler saw her eyes clench shut in the mirror. She felt her jerk and tense. And then she watched her come.

The noise was unlike anything Chandler had ever heard before. It was deep and dark and animal, primal right down to the marrow in her bones. It came up from Sarah for a long, long while, her body taut, holding to Chandler desperately, clutching her, ensuring that the pleasure would not escape.

The sound of it alone sent Chandler spinning into her own orgasm, her flesh screaming for Sarah's fingers, bearing down on the white cock in her hand. She thrust her head back and called out riding on the tail end of Sarah's and then laughing in ecstasy as Sarah bit down into the flesh of her shoulder once again.

"Oh, Sarah. Oh God, Sarah." She just couldn't stop saying

her name. She just couldn't stop coming. Knowing that Sarah had come, had let love in and let the pain go. Knowing that she'd trusted her enough to help her…the love alone…all of it hit her and forced every last nerve ending wide open. Her hand flew to Sarah's and she pressed against it, rubbing madly at her own flesh. "Sarah, Sarah, Sarah." She rubbed until the fireworks turned to sparks and her body jerked as each one extinguished for good.

"Fuck, yeah," she said, her body going slack against Sarah's. The white cock eased out of her, her muscles insisting.

"Mmm." Sarah hugged her tight and then released, her legs resting along the outside of Chandler's.

"I don't know about you, but, Jesus Christ, that was good."

Sarah nibbled on her ear. "You have no idea, Dr. Brogan."

Chandler kissed her hands and then pulled away slowly. Sarah sighed as the cock eased out of her. Facing her, Chandler sat on her knees and held her face. She searched her eyes, making sure she was okay.

"It was good?"

Sarah nodded and kissed her palm. "Oh, yeah."

Instantly, as quick as an orgasm comes and goes, Chandler wanted more. She envisioned herself atop her, thrusting into her beneath the covers, Sarah's hands clawing at her back and her legs wrapped around her waist.

Sarah raised an eyebrow, knowing she was thinking something.

"What's going on in there?"

Chandler grinned and her thumbs brushed at the diminishing shadows underneath her eyes.

"I want to take you again. Make love to you properly. Kiss your lips while you cry out in pleasure."

Sarah blinked slowly. Her lips started to move but stopped. "Soon, okay?"

Chandler kissed her, not ever wanting her to feel hesitant when it came to sharing her feelings.

"Okay." Moving to the side of the bed, Chandler stood and unbuckled the harness. She let it fall to her feet.

Just as she was about to extinguish the light, she saw a tear slip down Sarah's face.

"Hey," Chandler said, wiping it away gently. "We have all the time in the world."

"I know," Sarah said. "It's knowing that…it makes me feel so good. So…okay with everything. I never thought I would be here at this moment. I never thought I could trust someone or even trust myself. It's—all of it—it's incredible. And overwhelming."

Chandler sat next to her and held her hand. "You are truly amazing, do you know that? Your courage and your strength. Even your fear. I'm amazed by you, Sarah Monroe. And intrigued and in awe…and in love."

Sarah smiled.

"I love you too."

They kissed, slowly and softly and then Sarah spoke again. "Turn off that light, Dr. Brogan. Eternity starts now."

About the Author

Ronica Black spends her free time writing works that move her, with the hope that they will move others as well. She is a firm believer that "what does not kill you makes you stronger." Each step she takes in life is a journey meant to be experienced, whether it be a smooth step paved with green grass, or a rocky one marred with boulders. She keeps stepping, keeps writing, and keeps believing that women are far stronger than they believe. She's an award-winning author with four books currently published by Bold Strokes Books: In Too Deep, Deeper, Wild Abandon, and Hearts Aflame. She has short stories published in the Bold Strokes Books Erotic Interludes anthologies Stolen Moments, Lessons in Love, and Road Games. She was also published in Ultimate Lesbian Erotica 2005. Look for her upcoming book The Seeker to be released in December 2009, and her book Chasing Love, which will be released in 2010, both from Bold Strokes Books.

Bold Strokes
BOOKS
WEBSTORE
PRINT AND EBOOKS
Romance
Mystery
Intrigue
MATINEE BOOKS
BOLD STROKES BOOKS
Adventure
victory
EDITIONS
AEROS
BOOKS
Erotica
Fantasy
Sci-Fi
http://www.boldstrokesbooks.com